Love's Changes

A Losing My Way Novella

by

Love's Changes

Cover Artist: Taria A. Reed

Edited by: Gayla Leath

Disclaimer:

This is a work of fiction, any similarity to actual persons living or dead, products, businesses and locations are purely coincidental or used in a fictional manner.

This work of fiction contains adult content: depictions of sexual acts, explicit language that may be objectionable by some readers. This work is intended for adult audiences of 18 and older. Reader discretion is advised.

Dedication

To Damon (the hubbykins), Faith, Shyla, Heidi, Avril, Tyler, Jenna, & Damon (of the Suede persuasion): Thank you for helping me understand that I could do this.

To my weekly Twitter panel, Romance Writer Chat (#rwchat): Thank you for providing me with the keys to unlocking this novella writing business. This was absolute torture for someone as long-winded as me, but I made it through with your help.

To the Readers: Because you asked for Bryan and Justice's story. Thank you for loving these two just as much as I do.

Acknowledgements

To God, from whom all blessings flow, thank you for the gift, the desire, the support, and the opportunity. To Damon, this does not happen without you. Love you forever. To Sterling and Semaj, my heartbeats, the best parts of me. To my family and friends, thank you for putting up with my craziness.

To all of my JMC and LIJ people, your love strengthens me. To Damon, Faith, Heidi, Alexis, Robin, and Jenna, thank you for being conscientious and thorough beta readers. Your insight really helped me fashion this into something I'm proud of. To Gayla, I truly appreciate your help in shaping my crazy into something understandable. To my Loungers, you guys hold me down and keep me going. Thank you so much for the loyalty and encouragement.

To the readers, you will never know how much I have loved writing within this world that first began in my Queens of Kings series. Bryan and Justice were given their story only because you asked. Yeah, I know, I spoil y'all like that.

With Love & Heart,

~LaQuette~

Playlist

When I'm writing, music is a necessity that cannot be compromised. If the music isn't right, then the words won't flow. Here's a list of what was in my ears and in my heart while I was writing about these two wonderful men.

∞ Good Enough by Bobby Brown

∞ Freak'in Me by Jamie Foxx

∞ Digital Girl by Jamie Foxx

∞ Cry Me A River by Justin Timberlake

∞ Boogie Tonight by Tweet

∞ Blame it On the

Alcohol by Jamie Foxx

∞ Grind With Me by Pretty Ricky

∞ Hot Tottie by Usher ft. Jay Z

∞ I Like by Guy

∞ I know by Omarion

∞ I Like It by DeBarge

∞ I'm Tryna by Omarion

∞ Last Time by Trey Songz

∞ Losing My Way by Justin Timberlake

∞ My Body by LSG

∞ Right and a Wrong Way to Love Somebody by Keith Sweat

- ∞ Slow by Jamie Foxx
- ∞ Slow Motion by Trey Songz
- ∞ Stranger in Moscow by Michael Jackson
- ∞ Teach Me by Musiq Soulchild
- ∞ Today by Musiq Soulchild
- ∞ U Will Know by Black Men United
- ∞ What About Us by Brandy
- ∞ My Body by Tank
- ∞ Please Don't Go by Tank
- ∞ When by Tank
- ∞ The Show by Kelly Rowland ft. Tank

Love's Changes

A Losing My Way Novella

A near-fatal shot through his chest teaches Lieutenant Bryan Smyth of the NYPD two things: He wants to live to see more days and he wants to spend them with his estranged husband, Justice.

Poor decisions made under the strain of grief split the seams of their marriage. Now it's up to Bryan to show Justice there's still enough of their love left to salvage from the ruins, still something worth the battle ahead.

Bryan's shooting has opened Justice's eyes to new lessons too. The first, tomorrow isn't promised, the second, life's too short to live in misery. Justice has watched Bryan shuffle back and forth attempting to balance the man he is at home and the man he has to be at the precinct for too long. Now, he's done. The only problem is Justice's heart is having a hard time adhering to the exit strategy in his head.

Desperate to repair their bond, Bryan does the only thing he can to keep his marriage intact, he calls his crazy sister-in-law, True to stir up some organized chaos. She's a wildcard, yes. As unstable and deadly as nitroglycerin, but she gets the one thing Bryan needs more than anything, results.

The only question left: Is family and fidelity enough to get them through love's changes, or is this really the end?

Chapter 1

Bryan opened the door to the car and eased himself into the passenger seat…well, eased as much as he could considering his healed back-to-chest gunshot wound still throbbed like a son-of-a-bitch. His doctor called them phantom pains, the lingering reminder of a traumatic injury that victims sometimes experienced. Months after his injury he'd expected to be pain free. Too bad his body, or more likely his mind, just didn't seem to be on board with that idea.

When he was finally settled into the car, he leaned back against the headrest and released a long breath. Bryan felt the car dip as Justice slid into the driver's seat, yanked his seatbelt across his chest and secured it with one angry click.

"Everything okay?" Bryan asked as he reached across the console and placed a hand on Justice's thigh. Bryan was only permitted a brief second of contact when Justice pushed his hand away.

"I want a divorce, Bryan." Justice's matter-of-fact tone making it appear as if those particular words strung together were an everyday occurrence. "I've taken a temporary post at 6th Comm in Brooklyn. The Corps will let me stay there as long as it takes you to get through the next stage of your rehab. But after that I'm done and this is over."

Bryan flinched against the pain in his chest as he struggled to process Justice's words. When he was able to breathe past the pain, he turned to Justice.

"Just like that? You're leaving me? No explanation why?" Bryan's cracking voice sounded like metal scraping against itself. He was exerting so much focus keeping tears out of his eyes that Bryan forgot to clear his throat before he spoke. "Why, Justice?"

Justice kept his eyes fixed on the windshield, never sparing even the smallest of glances Bryan's way. It made Bryan's chest throb even more. The locked muscles in his husband's profile told Bryan just how much Justice was struggling, trying to keep from losing his shit.

"Jussy," Bryan whispered hoping Justice would understand the silent, *please don't do this*, that was knocking around in Bryan's heart.

"You know why. We both know why. I can't do this any longer, Bryan."

"Justice, please…just give me a chance to fix this. I can fix this—"

Justice shoved the key into the ignition, yanking the gearshift into drive. "I deserve better than living with a husband who's too ashamed to love himself, let alone love me where the rest of the world can see. You've had years to fix it, Bryan. You haven't, so I'm done."

***

Justice was leaving him.

Bryan stood in the shower replaying the brief, yet crippling conversation in the car.

Bryan gave himself a derisive laugh. Apparently being a decorated and skilled investigator didn't count for shit in marriage, because for damn sure he hadn't seen this one coming.

After five years of the on-again, off-again minefield they'd traversed, Justice was finally ready to walk away. It was ironic Bryan had been the one trying for years to get Justice to see their marriage wasn't salvageable. The very same divorce papers Justice threw in his face tonight were initially drafted at Bryan's request five years ago. Considering that fun-fact, he should be relieved Justice was finally seeing things clearly. Unfortunately, the only thing he seemed to be feeling was sick at the thought of losing his husband, especially now.

Coming very close to losing his life when he took a bullet to the chest while on duty, Bryan had a sudden urge to hold on to everything and everyone that meant anything to him. That piercing piece of metal in his chest was all it had taken to make Bryan realize leaving his husband wasn't the answer. Fighting for him was.

Just when his stupid ass was finally figuring things out, Justice wanted to up and bail.

How the fuck am I supposed to deal with that?

He wiped the water out of his stinging eyes; looking up to the ceiling for answers when a single thought crossed his mind.

You fight, that's how. You stop dicking around and get to the business of holding on to your man.

Dried, dressed, and determined, he walked down the long corridor of his Emerald Street apartment to find Justice bending down to get something out of the oven. He was wearing an A-line t-shirt and a pair of sweatpants. Nothing special, but on Justice's solid physique, it could have been a thong bikini for all Bryan's dick cared.

Down boy. Talking before loving, or it'll likely be just the two of us for a mighty long time.

He closed his eyes and took in a long breath of the aroma floating through the kitchen. The mix of sweet and savory scents gave his senses something other than the tasty curve of Justice's perfect ass to focus on.

"Mmm, smells so good," Bryan moaned. "Is that…?"

"Orange glazed pork chops with roasted potatoes and broccoli? Yeah. I figured if you're gonna begin training soon, you'd better enjoy food like this now. Whoever your trainer is, he's probably going to have you cutting down on carbs and fat for a while."

Bryan watched Justice carefully. His smooth caramel features, clean-shaven head and face kept him looking more youthful than his thirty-eight years. He was trying so hard to keep his tone normal and innocuous, but the tenseness he held in his shoulders was a clear sign of the emotional fight Bryan could see his husband enduring.

"Justice, aren't you training me?" Bryan's hope coloring the sound of his voice, making him sound just this side of desperate.

Justice moved their plates to the table and motioned for Bryan to join him. Once he complied, Justice tucked into his food and didn't lift his eyes until he was finished with his meal.

"I just don't think it's a good idea, Bryan. I think we both need to keep our distance, keep from allowing old feelings and habits to intrude on the decisions we're making now."

Bryan reached his hand across the table and carefully placed it atop Justice's. This was his husband, the man he'd sworn to love and cherish, the man he'd claimed as his own. The irony wasn't lost on him that he was sitting here silently begging for permission to touch what he'd had a license to touch for so long.

He'd done this. There was no doubt in Bryan's mind this was his fault. He just needed to know specifically what he'd done this time to fuck it all up.

"Why do you want a divorce now, Justice?"

Justice pushed his plate away and carefully wiped his mouth with a napkin.

"Because I'm tired of watching your shame eat you alive, Bryan. I'm tired of swimming in your river of guilt to try and save you. I can't do it anymore. We've been together since we were seventeen. After twenty-one years together, at what point are you going to feel comfortable enough with yourself that you can admit to the world and your precious NYPD that you're gay and married to a man? "

Justice was angry. His tight features and biting sarcasm was proof enough of his feelings. But more than that, Bryan detected something else that hurt so much more than Justice's anger: Justice's sadness.

Chapter 2

Bryan swallowed as he removed his hand from Justice's. Both he and Justice had come to their sexual identities in vastly different ways. Justice came from this overwhelmingly supportive family that loved him and accepted him just as he was. Even his devoutly religious and ultra-macho heteronormative father, General Amare, didn't seem to mind the fact that his youngest son loved and married a man.

If the world were full of more people like the Amares, then no child would ever battle with their ability to accept themselves. Justice certainly drew the long straw when it came to the gay kid's parent lotto. If only Bryan had been that fortunate.

After seventeen years of living in his bigoted father's house, Bryan knew one thing, a gay son was something his father would never tolerate. Bryan didn't need to ask the question to be convinced of that answer in his mind.

When Bryan was certain of who he was inside, he knew instantly he could never live under his father's roof and still be his authentic self. He'd worked hard in school to get scholarships. His hope was to attend school in a more progressive part of the country, a place where the small-mindedness of the conservative South couldn't affect him.

A few more months was all he'd needed to be free. He was going to school in New York; there would be no one there to dictate how he could live, whom he could love.

A five minute lapse in judgement, a persistent prick who wouldn't take no for an answer, and a blow job, were all it had taken to destroy his dreams.

Uzziah Conway barged into his home one night while Bryan's parents were at their weekly prayer meeting. Awkward and unskilled in the manner of social graces, Bryan hadn't stood a chance of turning down the town troublemaker with those hypnotic gray eyes.

All these years later Bryan couldn't really remember how he'd ended up against the wall with his pants around his ankles and his dick down Uzziah's throat, but the moment he'd felt the slide of those lips around his cock, Bryan's brain tapped out and his bottled up sexuality took over.

Those few stupid moments of weakness robbed Bryan of everything he'd worked so hard for up to that point. After experiencing his first orgasm that hadn't come from his own hand, he opened his eyes to find his parents standing in the living room in shock.

His father beat him mercilessly that night. And when Bryan awoke, he'd shipped him off to the nearest Marine recruitment center. Bryan had two choices, join the Marines and become a *real* man, or die at his father's hand.

A part of Bryan's soul died as he signed those papers, and what remained of it barely made it through basic training. But something unexpected happened after he'd come through the fire of basic training. He'd stumbled upon a smiling Marine that would change the course of his life.

Justice had smiled at Bryan like he knew him, *really* knew him. There was never a moment where he had to disclose to Justice who he was, Justice just seemed to know.

The smiling Marine had loved Bryan at a pace that was comfortable for him and then taken Bryan home and shared the wonderful gift of the Amare family. After that, Bryan knew he'd love Justice Amare for the rest of his life.

He'd vowed as much on their wedding day. To have and to hold, 'til death us do part. That was his pledge. Yet he was sitting here now pissing away everything they'd built because he couldn't find his way out of the damn maze they were in.

"I can't lose you," Bryan barked, the rage in his voice evidence of nothing more than how angry he was with himself. "I won't lose you."

Justice watched him carefully, as if waiting for the rest of whatever Bryan intended to say to spill from his lips. Bryan knew something should follow the declaration he'd just made, but he couldn't find the words.

When have you ever needed words to communicate with the man you love?

Bryan walked around the table until he was standing behind Justice. He let a slow hand drift from Justice's shoulder sliding down the front of his ribbed tee. When his fingers grazed against his husband's nipple, Bryan delighted in the quick intake of breath Justice pulled in through clenched teeth.

Bryan leaned down and licked a wet strip up the side of his man's neck until he reached the rough patch of stubble just beneath Justice's angled jaw. He smiled; it was so rare he actually had the chance to feel stubble on Justice. Being a career Marine, meant Bryan's man was clean-shaven all the time. Feeling the burn of the closest thing Bryan had ever seen to a beard on Justice made his dick twitch.

He found Justice's full lips waiting for him. They met the press of Bryan's with equal pressure and excitement, teeth clinking and tearing at each other's flesh. He held Justice's upturned face with one hand, and allowed the other to travel down the length of Justice's torso, beyond his abdomen until he was grasping the hefty bulge of a thick cock and full balls.

Bryan gave a gentle squeeze to his bounty and smiled against a hungry mouth when the anticipated moan crossed his husband's lips.

"Let's not figure this out tonight. I need you…please," Bryan begged.

Justice pulled away from Bryan. He didn't take long to contemplate Bryan's request, just stood and led Bryan by the hand to their bedroom.

Once there Justice removed his clothing in a few quick motions and lay across the foot of their bed on his back. He planted one foot on the bed and began stroking himself. Bryan could never tell whose benefit it was for when Justice jacked himself off in front of Bryan. He was certain Justice received pleasure from it, but nothing made Bryan want to bust a nut like watching his man rub one out in front of him.

Bryan's gaze focused on the strong fingers that were wrapped around the proud cock between his husband's legs. A darker shade of caramel than the rest of him, thick and long, glistening with some of the pre-cum Justice must've captured on his last upstroke.

Soon Justice was pumping his hips in time with his strokes. If Bryan wanted in on this action he'd better get in now or it would be too late.

"What position are you playing tonight?" Both he and Justice enjoyed switching. Flip fucking was their specialty, each giving and taking until they were too exhausted to do more than collapse.

"I'm where I want to be," Justice replied. Bryan nodded and reached in the nightstand. In one pass of his he Bryan had both the lube and a condom in his grip, tossing them next to Justice's thigh. He squeezed a generous amount of the lube on his fingers, rubbing it between them to add a little warmth before he let it slide down his lover's taint. He climbed onto the bed between his man's legs, letting his fingers trail from the bottom of Justice's sack to the dark, puckered skin pulsing in anticipation of Bryan's touch.

There'd been too much time since he had the ability to touch his husband like this. Justice splayed out on their bed waiting in expectancy for Bryan's touch was a thing of beauty. It was something Bryan never tired of.

Bryan rubbed his fingers against the wrinkled surface of Justice's hole and delighted in the sensual quiver that moved down his body. Bryan started a smooth circular motion with his fingers providing just enough pressure to help loosen the muscle. Taking a glance at Justice's eyes he could see fire blazing under hooded lids. Bryan knew what Justice wanted, it was what his husband always wanted, Bryan's mouth wrapped around his cock.

Before the night was through Bryan would make certain Justice had what he wanted, but right now Bryan needed to make Justice want it just a little bit more. He pointed the tip of his tongue and pressed it into the junction where thigh met crotch. He continued his path upward allowing his tongue to travel up to Justice's bellybutton, across the ripple of his hardened abs, between the valley of his pecs, until he found a hard nub standing at attention for him.

The sight of those pert peaks had Bryan moaning before he could even take his first taste. He licked one nub and then the other, loving the feel and flavor of them on his tongue. He closed his lips tightly around one and let his teeth graze the flesh there.

Justice's cock and ass were always so sensitive; a cool breeze running across either could make him hard enough to cut granite. If massaging those areas was the quickest way to get his man ready for lovemaking, then loving on his nipples was a close second.

Bryan teased the nipple with his teeth, as he gently slid his fingers into the tight sheath of Justice's hole. The tight squeeze Justice gave him in response made Bryan ache to be where his fingers were. He knew what it was to be engulfed completely in Justice's heat. It was more addictive than any drug, more powerful than anything he'd ever encountered in his life. The need to be there, joined with his man overrode all common sense.

Bryan began to stroke slowly inside of Justice, twisting and spreading his fingers. He moved up to meet his husband's full lips, loving the feel of them beneath his. Bryan pressed deeper into the kiss allowing his lips to mimic the motion and the rhythm of his fingers. Justice's body was humming, as if silently asking Bryan for more.

Bryan pulled away from the kiss and caught sight of something unfamiliar in Justice's eyes. After more than two decades together Bryan knew his cues. Right now his eyes should be glazed over with need and desire. Right now every part of Justice's body should be begging Bryan for satisfaction. In truth his body was doing just that, tight muscles clenched around Bryan's fingers, breath coming in tufts of air, hand stroking long and fast up his cock, those were all appropriate responses to Bryan's ministrations. But even though the physical was there, his eyes told another story.

In Justice's eyes, there was hesitation. Not anxious anticipation, but hesitation mixed with fear.

"What's wrong?" They'd been together long enough that Bryan would've known if Justice was in pain. This wasn't about pain, or at least it wasn't about the physical kind. "Justice, do you want me to stop?"

Chapter 3

Justice tried hard to focus on Bryan's words. The fingers in his ass and the hard dick between his legs made that a difficult task. He blinked until Bryan's face became clear in his field of vision.

"I always want to make love to you, Bryan," he whispered as he leaned up and pressed a soft kiss against his husband's lips.

"Then what's wrong?" Bryan's forehead wrinkled with concern as his deep brown eyes raked over Justice's face. "Because something is definitely wrong."

"Is this really the time to discuss this, with your fingers up my ass and my dick leaking on my stomach?"

Bryan watched him carefully, his smooth features marred by worry. Soon Justice felt his fingers begin to retreat. He stilled Bryan's movements with a firm grip to Bryan's arm.

"Don't," he commanded.

"Then tell me what's wrong."

Justice took a deep breath and relaxed as best he could. This wasn't the most opportune time to have a discussion, but losing the opportunity to have Bryan satisfy him wasn't an option he was really willing to consider at this point.

"I always want you to touch me, Bryan. I just wonder if we should. This is not going to fix things. Might just make things worse."

Justice felt Bryan's fingers begin to move again. Rubbing against the walls of his channel, making the sensitive nerves there come alive. Justice's body spasmed involuntarily, delighting in the feel of being stroked from the inside out.

"I know it's not going to fix anything, Justice. But after all we've lost and me being shot...I just want us to feel good, baby," Bryan's desire poured from his lips in that soft deep rumble that Justice loved so much.

Bryan changed the angle of his fingers, rubbing against Justice's prostate, garnering a full body quiver from Justice. He added a third finger to Justice's passage, opening him up, stretching him, making him feel so full and yet still not fulfilled.

"Don't we deserve to feel good for a change, Jussy?"

The last five years of their relationship had been the most challenging of the twenty-one years they'd been together. It seemed as if the first sixteen years were perfect, and the moment they'd legally tied the knot, life decided to take all of their happiness away.

Dealing with Bryan's being closeted at work, losing their little girl, Bryan being shot and nearly killed in the line of duty, Justice always being gone on dangerous deployments; it was more than enough to destroy the best of couples.

They loved each other fiercely; Justice had no doubt about this. But they'd also hurt each other too. Lately it seemed as if they were always trying to heal from some fresh round of hell life had inflicted upon them. After being burdened with so much heartache Justice could only find one answer to Bryan's question.

"Hell yeah," Justice choked out, his senses on fire, thirsty for the promise of satisfaction Bryan's fingers were tapping out against his sensitive spot.

Justice wrapped strong fingers around Bryan's neck and pulled him into a firm kiss. Lips slammed hard and fast against each other, letting his man know he was exactly where he wanted to be, doing exactly what he wanted to be doing.

Bryan smiled against his lips before pulling away. He moved down the length of his body creating a trail of kisses. When Bryan met the hard cock lying fat and heavy against Justice's abdomen, he placed a gentle kiss on its swollen head. The sensation of Bryan's lips on his cock made Justice twitch with anticipation and need.

Bryan circled the cap slowly with his tongue, taking a moment to scoop the pearl of pre-cum from his slit. Justice tugged on his own balls trying to stave off his orgasm as long as he could. This was just the tip of the iceberg. If he gave into his growing need to come now, he'd never experience the blessed heat of Bryan's wet, hot mouth wrapped around him.

"Please," Justice begged.

The corner of Bryan's mouth lifted in a crooked smile and made Justice's dick weep. That smile meant Bryan was going to try to break him, and God help him, Justice was going to welcome him doing so.

Bryan opened his mouth and took Justice's cock in one long swallow, straight to the back of his throat. The result was Justice clenching his ass around Bryan's fingers trying hard not to lose his fucking load.

Bryan cupped his tongue and let it caress the underside of Justice's dick. The dual stimulation of tongue on cock and fingers in ass had every muscle in his body locked in an effort to keep him from going over the edge.

Bryan bobbed a few more times up and down on Justice's pulsing rod, pulling his already tightened sack up even further. He took one last slow lick from base to tip before he pulled off of Justice's cock.

Bryan moved away long enough to remove his clothes and pick up the condom and the tube of slick lying beside Justice.

"Do you want me to?"

Bryan's question hung heavy in the air. He held the foil packet between his thumb and pointer finger, waiting for Justice to answer. Justice trusted Bryan with his life, despite all of the bullshit Bryan had put them through, he never questioned Bryan's fidelity.

"Is there a reason I should ask my husband to wear one?"

"Never," Bryan's answer was quick.

Bryan added more lube in and around Justice's ass, quickly coating his cock with the remainder. Usually watching Bryan undress was part of the process, the seduction. It was one of the things that got him so hot he'd be begging for pretty much anything Bryan wanted to do to him by the end.

But tonight he was so on edge. Who was he fooling? When it came to Bryan, Justice was always on edge. Their physical time together was usually few and far between. With Bryan's duties as an NYPD lieutenant and Justice's service in the Marine Corps, there was often precious little time the two had to share. As a result, whenever they were face-to-face, flesh-to-flesh, body-to-body, there was always this soul-penetrating need to have as much of each other as time and their endurance would allow.

Bryan positioned himself at Justice's entrance, the domed head of his cock pressing gently against Justice's taint. The gentle pressure made Justice ache for the sensuous ride he knew Bryan was going to give him. Justice wrapped sure fingers around the back of Bryan's neck, latching onto his lips. Pressing and biting so hard he expected to taste the coppery tang of blood on his tongue.

Somewhere between him attacking Bryan's lips and his next ragged breath, Bryan was seated balls-deep inside of him. Justice felt like he was choking on a myriad of sensations. With Bryan's hot, firm tongue in his mouth, and hard cock in his ass, he was so full, so stuffed, yet so desperate.

Bryan pried his lips away from Justice, giving them the opportunity to take in needed air. Didn't matter that Justice's lungs were on fire burning for life's breath. The moment those lips left his, he was mewling like a hungry babe.

Justice heard the needy moan leave his lips. But before his brain could form words to indicate his body's desires, Bryan was pulling back leaving only the tip of his cock inside Justice.

Only a brief second passed before Bryan was gliding back in again. He pressed one long stroke in, another out and then in again, each increasing in pace and power. Within a couple of strokes Bryan was giving Justice the ride he was so desperately in need of.

Heavy balls were smacking against Justice's taint, the curved ridge of Bryan's cock stroking out the perfect rhythm against his prostate, his own cock leaking on his abdomen. God how he loved this, the way they were together, the perfect way their bodies always knew just what to do to bring the other joy. If only they could duplicate this connectivity, the ability to be perfectly in sync with one another in the real world and not just in their bedroom.

Justice wrapped tight but careful fingers around his sack. He could feel his testicles drawing up against his body making way for a release he knew was going to be both powerful and frenzied.

He wasn't ready to come yet. He needed this to last a little bit longer. He needed that fucking cock to stretch him, fill him, conquer him in the worst way.

Bryan must have realized Justice was edging toward the end. He pulled out leaving Justice's hole aching to be filled again. "Turn over," the deep baritone of Bryan's voice was vibrating throughout the room, making Justice's body tremble without the benefit of touch.

Justice scurried onto all fours, eager to have his husband's sizable cock inside him again. Without preamble Bryan was planted right back where Justice wanted him. This time he was deeper, seemingly hitting every nerve in his channel as he pushed forward and slid back.

On his last downward stroke, Bryan locked strong fingers around Justice's shoulders and rammed himself as deeply as either of their bodies would allow. Justice planted his face in the pillow gritting his teeth as Bryan's punishing rhythm bordered on the fine threshold between ecstasy and pain.

"Shit, I'm there," Justice wailed.

"Good, so am I."

Balls tight and achy, Justice felt fire travel from somewhere deep inside of him. Muscles locked, fingers buried into the mattress, his untouched cock spewed jets of milky cum all over the bed beneath his still spasming body.

Justice felt Bryan's thick and long cock pulse inside of him. His shoulders nearly succumbing to the increasing pressure of Bryan's iron clasp. Justice fell forward and Bryan's snapping hips followed him refusing to leave his battered hole until his release was completed.

Bodies still coming down off of the sexed out high, lungs fighting to drag in air, Justice could almost forget that everything wasn't fine, that things hadn't changed. Justice was halfway near to post fuck sleep when he heard Bryan's half-cry, half-whisper, "Please don't go."

And just like that they were right back in the middle of this fucked up situation they currently found themselves in.

Chapter 4

Bryan knew he was alone. Before he opened his eyes, before he turned over and felt cool sheets on Justice's side of the bed and looked at the glaringly empty spot beside him, Bryan knew his husband was gone.

They'd connected last night. The way Justice touched Bryan, the way Justice allowed Bryan to touch him in return, it wasn't all about sexual release. Yet he was lying in their marriage bed alone.

"I can't do this shit anymore. I'm not losing my man to this bullshit."

Bryan rolled out of bed, determined to set things right in both his work and his home life. After all these years on the force, the only person who knew anything about his life and his love, was his boss.

"Shit's gotta change."

He showered and pulled on some sweats and sneakers before he got in his car. He winced as his muscles reminded him of last night's activities. He ignored the discomfort. He needed to head to work. He needed to get there and…

Do what? Land yourself in the exact same position as Madison?

He slowed down and entered the parking lot behind the precinct, a sense of uneasiness biting at the base of his skull as he pulled into his designated parking spot.

Fifteen years on the force and he'd built a career he could be proud of. He protected his community. He was respected by his colleagues and the people he safeguarded. That wasn't an easily accomplished task. The seventy-fourth had the highest crime rates in all of Brooklyn. Being responsible for both Brownsville and East New York combined, two of the poorest areas in the borough, made it nearly impossible to do his job. But he did it, got results, and still managed to keep his humanity intact.

But those same homies on the corner that gave him dap when they saw him might not be so inclined to embrace Bryan if they knew who he loved. The brass in NYPD that pinned so many medals on him throughout his career might not be so quick to sing Bryan's praises if they knew who Bryan really was.

Madison had done it. Albeit unintentionally, he'd done it. He was seeing someone in the Brooklyn D.A.'s office. They'd gone to a movie out in Westbury, Long Island, figuring they were far enough away from work to avoid any awkward run-ins. They were holding hands, not kissing, not hugging up, not doing anything overtly sexual, when they ran into a cop from the seventy-fourth.

Before Madison could return to work, his secret was already fodder for the in-house gossips.

A week later while out on a call, Madison was separated from his partner and ended up beaten nearly to death. He'd called dispatch for backup, dispatch sounded the alarm, but strangely enough, help didn't arrive until it was way too late.

Bryan was the lead detective on that investigation. He remembered going to the hospital and looking at the pummeled flesh that looked more like ground meat than a human face. He remembered the red gashes coated in rusty dried blood that seemed to be over every inch of skin the man had.

Those images and that case haunted Bryan still to this day. Hell, every time he walked into the precinct and saw Madison sitting at the front desk—because that was the only job Madison could do after the attack—Bryan was reminded of what his fate could be if he made the same mistake. Bryan's fear compelled him to keep his personal life away from anyone that had any affiliation with his work.

But Justice needs you to fix this…

He felt fortified again, just the thought of his husband gave him enough strength to get out of the car and push through the doors.

Bryan's heart beat faster, but despite the extra adrenaline running through his system he was determined to give Justice what he needed. He made it as far as the front desk when Madison's hollow blue eyes looked up and met with Bryan's gaze.

Empty, sad, beaten, and broken. That's what Madison was.

And that's what you'll be too if you let these people know shit about who you are.

Bryan turned around on his heel before anyone could notice him and headed right back to his car. The minute he'd sworn he was taking to compose himself, turned into five. When he couldn't get his heart rate under control, Bryan put the car in gear and headed toward his apartment. It wasn't until the key was in his door, and he was pushing into the safety of his apartment that his senses dulled, his heart slowed down, and his fear subsided.

"Maybe Justice is right; maybe I'm too much of a coward to deserve someone like him."

***

Justice gritted his teeth as he tried to balance the heavy barbell above his chest on shaky arms. Usually he bench pressed twice as much weight as he currently had in his hands right now. But with his mind and his heart out of sync and out of focus, it was hard for him to balance the weight.

"Are you fucking crazy? You know better than to try to lift that much without somebody here to fucking spot you."

The boom of Law's voice filled the room, making Justice's arms shake a little more. Before Justice could argue, his oldest brother gripped the barbell and lifted it out of his hands and back onto its safety rack.

"What's wrong, Justice?"

Justice shook his head as he sat up and wheezed out a quick, "Nothing."

Law crossed his arms over his chest and leaned back casually against the wall, his skepticism evident in the side eye he was giving Justice right now.

"Bullshit, I was there when you were born and I know everything there is to know about your fucking ass. You's a lie. What's going on?"

Law took a look around the open landscape of the gym in their father's basement. "Where is Bryan? Isn't he supposed to begin his training today?"

Justice nodded, "Yeah. He's coming by later…after I leave."

"Aren't you training him?" When Justice shook his head, Law continued to question him. "Why not?"

"Because I'm divorcing him."

"You say what, now?" The base in his brother's voice making the baby brother in Justice tremble just slightly.

Justice stepped away from his brother's piercing gaze and walked over to get a drink from his water bottle. He kept his eyes focused on the bottle, kept his mind focused on the task at hand: open bottle, lift bottle, pour water, and swallow. He knew explaining this to his family was going to be just as hard as explaining it to Bryan. Hell he could barely understand it himself.

They'd loved each other since they were children playing at being men in Uncle Sam's Marine Corps. He never imagined a day they wouldn't be together, or more importantly wouldn't want to be together. Things had changed these last five years. The most significant of those changes was the gaping wound in their foundation left by their daughter's death.

Justice loved Bryan. There was no doubt about that. But loving someone and being able to stand by and watch them destroy themselves day by day was something Justice wasn't sure he could do anymore.

Thinking back on it now, Justice could almost remember the exact moment the change happened.

They were happy; happier than any couple had the right to be. They'd finally married, finally made honest men of one another after being together for so long. They stood before God and man and declared their love for one another. And then shortly afterward they decided to expand their family.

Justice was one of four. His siblings were everything to him. The Amare family was tight. They didn't let a lot of outsiders in, but when they did, they loved them as their own. From the moment Justice brought Bryan home, he was theirs. Justice had so many dreams of bringing forth the next generation of Amare children who would continue the legacy of loving and leaning on one another for life. To that, fate had another plan set in place.

They were happy throughout their surrogate's pregnancy, every event unfolding with almost textbook like precision. Until one day when everything went wrong. The surrogate hadn't felt the baby move. They rushed her to the hospital, but it was too late. Their little girl was gone.

They'd been there for the agonizing birth. The silent operating room heavy with sorrow, only the beeping sounds of the monitor filling the void. And when it was all over, the kind nurse swaddled the stillborn infant and placed her in Bryan's arms.

The official cause of death was a rare genetic mutation with some long complicated name that Justice to this day still couldn't pronounce. Something that went undetected for the entire pregnancy had robbed them of the greatest joy of their lives.

Justice knew there was nothing that could've saved their daughter. But somewhere in the back of Bryan's mind he began to believe that he was the problem. After all, that's what Bryan's mother instilled in him. It was his sin—homosexuality—that killed their baby girl. Once that little piece of poison slipped past Bryan's logical brain, it began to poison the whole of him, eating at him, filling him with so much guilt he could hardly stand to get out of bed in the morning. Somehow the guilt became so toxic and pervasive. Bryan began withdrawing himself from everyone he loved, including Justice.

How do you fight that? How do you, the person on the outside, battle someone else's internal demons?

Justice didn't have the answer then and he certainly didn't have it now. But after watching Bryan nearly die in a hospital bed he knew that he couldn't spend the next five, ten, or thirty years of his life watching Bryan's guilt do what that bullet hadn't, slowly kill him.

"You can't be serious?" Law's voice pulled Justice out of his journey down a very dark memory.

"I'm tired, Law." Justice sat down on the floor, his surrender evident in a long sigh. "He's never going to forgive himself. He's always going to believe the crap his mother poured into his head. He's always going to believe that our daughter's death was a punishment from God because of who we love and how we love. How does an openly gay man believe some nonsense like that?"

Law sat down next to Justice, lightly bumping his shoulder. A move meant to tell him his big brother was there for him. "Justice, he loves you. Bryan is not ashamed of you or the life you share. He's also not had it as easy as you have. Bryan didn't have a family that loved him enough to accept him as he was. It takes a long time to completely break free of something like that.

"He's finally in a place where he's moving beyond that, breaking through his guilt and grief, and you want to leave him now? That's not what family does, Justice. You should know that, you had a better example of that than Bryan did. You don't give up on family. You fight for them, until the last breath."

Uncomfortable tension moving throughout him, Justice rolled his shoulders and neck. That was his brother's intention, to make him uncomfortable. But regardless of Law's attempt at laying guilt at Justice's feet, he knew the truth. Standing by Bryan, watching the man you love slowly kill himself, was something Justice could not do.

***

Bryan felt his phone vibrate in his pocket. A smile bloomed on his face as he saw his oldest brother-in-law's name flash across the screen.

"'Sup, Law?"

"Nothing much." Law's succinct answer was a typical reply from his brother-in-law. Not one for drawing things out, Law's conversations were the epitome of short and sweet. "I heard you're looking for a new trainer. Is that right?"

Resignation filled him. Justice had revealed his plans to the family. Keeping anything from the Amare family was unlikely. They were extremely close knit and they kept in contact at a ridiculous rate considering they were usually all scattered throughout different parts of the world on some form of military mission or another. He should have known they'd be privy to his husband's recent decision to end their marriage.

"So I guess Justice told you he's planning to divorce me?"

"He did," Law's quick answer scraping against Bryan's heart. "I'm just calling to find out if that's what you want too."

Bryan stood there shaking his head for a moment before he realized he needed to verbally respond to Law's inquiry. "No, I don't. But after pushing Justice away for so many years, I don't really know if I have the right to fight him on this decision."

"He loves you, Bryan. That is what's most important. If you really want to keep your husband and your marriage intact, that's the only thing you need to focus on. Now as I hear it, you need someone to train you and my bonehead brother has refused to do it."

"He did refuse me. As much as I love him, the training part is about more than him. I really do have to get right again if I'm going back on the force to be more than a desk jockey." Bryan's skin prickled at the thought of being locked behind his desk for the rest of his career.

"All right." Law's answer seemed so simplistic considering the topic of their conversation. "I'm going to give you the perfect substitute, but I have to do one thing first."

"What's that?" Bryan asked.

"Call True."

Bryan shook his head. True was the youngest sibling and only sister in the Amare clan. As such, she ran the Amare family like a strict task master. Didn't shit go down without her knowledge and approval.

"No offense, Law, but you know your sister is crazy. Is she even on this side of the country right now?"

"She's in DC debriefing from her last mission. She's laying over in New York for a few days on her way back home to L.A."

"Law, I say again, we both know your sister is crazy."

Law laughed a little bit. Bryan knew damn well the man shared the same assessment of the lone female child of the Amare family. She was brilliant, that was for sure, but she was extremely unpredictable. As volatile as Justice seemed to be at this moment, when it came to their relationship Bryan wasn't sure he wanted to add his crazy ass sister-in-law into the mix.

"It's true, she is," Law agreed as he continued laughing on the other end of the phone. "But we both know the one thing she does better than anyone else in this family is get results. And I'm kind of thinking since your husband is talking about divorcing you, you want results."

Bryan had to think this through. One false move and he could end up a single man again. Truth was, if there was anyone in this family that could get his man to see straight, it was True Amare.

Bryan released a long, acquiescing breath. "I'm desperate, man. I guess I don't really have much choice." The truth of his situation pressing heavily on his heart. His life was fucked up, and if he didn't do something drastic, it just might remain that way.

"You're family Bryan, and we always take care of family. We got you. We got both of you."

If there was one thing Bryan believed in it was the power of the Amare family. They took care of their own. And he was certain he was one of theirs.

"Thanks man," Bryan's feeble reply masking the magnitude of his appreciation.

"Meet me at Pops' house first thing tomorrow morning," Law stated. "We are going to show my little brother how much he really doesn't want to leave his man."

Chapter 5

Justice stood at the stove watching the bubbling casserole he just pulled from the oven. Baked macaroni and cheese was his favorite comfort food. He didn't eat it often. Way too much cheese and pasta, but when he was feeling bad, it was the first thing his taste buds asked for.

He was feeling bad. His husband was home alone in their apartment while Justice was roaming the halls of his father's house by himself. His other siblings were either out of town or on the prowl. Either way the end result was Justice was staring at a dish full of cheesy goodness and trying to remind himself that eating it all would only lend him more time in the gym.

"Fuck it."

He grabbed a large serving spoon and a plate, digging a massive hole in the center of the dish. He was just about to take the serving spoon and shove the large piece of cutlery into his mouth when he felt the presence of another in the kitchen. He looked up to find his sister, True, leaning against the doorway, arms and ankles crossed, eyebrow lifted, and most likely a smart ass comment waiting behind curved lips.

"Go ahead. Be my guest," she cooed. "Have all those damn carbs, all that fat. Just give me an excuse to run your ass through PT." She was laughing at him, yeah. But he knew damn well she meant every single one of those words spilling out of her mouth.

"What are you even doing here?" Waiting for his sister to strike was never the best technical move. Cutting her off at the knees before she had a chance to attack was the only way to grasp at any hope of avoiding her assaults. "Thought you're supposed to be on mission somewhere?"

"I was. It's finished. I got a few days before my next patient is due in surgery in LA, so I decided to come spend a few days with Pops and any of my siblings that might be hanging around."

She walked into the middle of the kitchen, pulled open the silverware drawer, and removed a spoon. She dug the spoon into the center of his plate and hummed once she had a mouthful of his food. "That's damn good, Justice. Now tell me, who you mad at?"

Justice rolled his eyes as he turned for the refrigerator. He needed something cold to wash down all the grease he was about to inhale. That was the thing with the Amare children; they all had this uncanny connection, always knowing when something was right or wrong with the others.

Knowing there was always someone to pull him out of a hole if he needed it, that had his back at all times, inspired a confidence in Justice that kept his emotions on an even keel. But having his family all up in his business right now, when his life was blowing up into little pieces, really wasn't what he wanted or needed.

He put his plate down on a nearby counter and opened the fridge.

"Not mad at anybody, just hungry."

He grabbed a cold beer, popped it open, and took a long swig.

Just great. A plate full of fatty carbs, and beer.

This eating his feelings bullshit had to stop, either that or he was going to catch hell his next round of PT fitness tests.

He stared at the beer bottle as he waited for his sister to say something. That's what True did; she saw something, she said something. After a few moments of silence he turned in expectation. Still nothing, she simply nodded her head and said, "A'ight."

She walked past him and clapped him on the back as she made her way out of the kitchen. "I've had a rough couple of days, I'm going to bed. I'm supposed to be meeting one of my occupational therapists in the morning to discuss giving him a ride back to LA."

"One of your employees came to New York without a way to get back home to LA?"

"Nah, he's a new hire. I've worked with him over the years through the Corps and now that he's retiring, I gave him a job at Trinity. He was in DC tying up some loose ends to be processed out. He'll be here first thing in the morning. When I leave he's copping a ride back with me."

She made it halfway through the doorway before he turned around and said, "Want me to fix you a plate?"

She shook her head, "No. You know once Pops finds out I'm here he's gonna have me downstairs in that damn gym. Not trying to feel like hell on a stick while he's making me drop and give him one hundred."

Uncertainty niggled at the base of his neck as he watched her walk away. Maybe his sister was finally learning to mind her own business? Probably not, but he was too tired to be bothered by it now.

"I'm going to eat my food and drink my beer and that's all," he took another swig of his beer to validate his point. Tomorrow be damned, divorce be damned, he was just going to enjoy this moment right here. Tomorrow would handle itself.

Chapter 6

Bryan tapped on the acrylic pane on his Captain's office door. She was currently slumped over reading something on her desk, looking like misery warmed over by death. He chuckled a little at the administrative papers he had in his hands that required her signature.

She'll be happy to see these added to the pile.

"Come in," her eyes never left whatever document she was reading as she waved him into the room.

"I've been gone for months and you can't even spare me a glance? Damn, show a brother some kind of love."

Heart kept her eyes on her desk, but he could see her full rounded cheeks rise in amusement.

"So you've been off for months scratching your ass and I'm supposed to throw you a party every time you set foot in my precinct?"

Talking shit with his friend, his captain, brought back happier times. This job, this house, this woman had kept him sane through some of the darker moments of his life. It wasn't lost on him that he was standing here in her office now when things in his world seemed to be spiraling out of control in his personal life.

She motioned for him to take a seat in front of her desk. "What brings you down here?

"I can't just want to see my favorite captain?"

"I might be the youngest captain in NYPD history, but that doesn't mean I'm naïve. What brings you down?"

He lifted the large yellow envelope in his hand. "Some paperwork HR needs you to fill out and sign so I can keep getting those big checks NYPD sends in the mail."

She couldn't hold her loud laughter in on that one. Yeah they made decent salaries as admins in the department, but they certainly weren't reflective of the amount of work or the risks they took protecting and serving the community. Police work was a thankless job; you did it because you believed in it, not because you were looking to get something out of it.

"You could have faxed or mailed that to me. You know as soon as I saw it I would have filled it out and gotten it back to you. I don't play with stuff like this. My people won't go without because of a paperwork fuck up on my end. Does your visit have anything to do with my cousin deciding to leave you?"

Bryan heaved a long breath into the air. "Is there anyone in your family that doesn't know every detail of my business?"

She shook her head with an almost regrettable smile. "You know how it goes in the Amare clan. We're all connected better than any cellphone or communications company out there. Free is off in a jungle somewhere halfway across the world and he sent me a message asking about the two of you."

All Bryan could do was shake his head. He didn't doubt his husband's second older brother had some very strong opinions about his current marital situation. They all did, and they were all pretty vocal about their opinions too.

"What's Free saying?"

Heart shrugged as she tapped out a quick rhythm on her desk with her fingers. "The same as the rest of us, that you guys need to figure this shit out before anyone gets hurt beyond what they already are. We love you both, Bryan. We don't want to see either of you hurting."

Bryan's chest felt tight. These people did love him, despite all the pain he'd brought to Justice's life.

He was about to speak when he felt his phone vibrating in his pocket. He handed her the packet of paperwork, and stepped out of her door before answering.

"Justice? Is everything okay?"

"I need to meet with you, are you free?"

Justice's voice was filled with urgency. A small drop of hope filled Bryan's heart. His man was reaching out to him. That had to be a good sign, right? If Justice hated Bryan, if he were still determined to go through with this divorce, he wouldn't be on the phone telling Bryan he *needed* him, would he?

It was a leap for sure, but Bryan could hear his husband's late grandmother Ida-Mae Amare saying to him, "Faith as big as a mustard seed can move mountains. You just gotta believe, boy." That was one wise old woman and Bryan preferred to lean on her wisdom rather than his fear.

"I'm at the precinct dropping off some papers. Can I meet you somewhere?"

"Nah, I'm not too far from there. Give me fifteen and I'll meet you inside your office."

The line was dead after Justice's brief edict. Bryan pushed open Heart's door again and stepped inside.

"Is my office still my office? Your cousin just asked to drop by."

"What did he want?"

Bryan shook his head. He'd like to know the answer to that question as well. It wasn't like Justice to be secretive. When he didn't want to answer something, he didn't. He didn't feel the need to be sneaky about most things, which was strangely surprising considering the cloak and dagger world he lived in while working military intelligence.

"He didn't say, just asked if we could meet."

"Grazzo is using your office because I need him to. Once you come back he'll be right back in the squad room."

"He there now?"

She shook her head no and dismissed him with a slight wave of her hand. Bryan stepped into the hall and bumped into a large mass. He looked up to find Sergeant Madison in front of him.

"Lieutenant Smyth? You're back?" Madison seemed surprised.

"Not yet, I just needed some papers signed by Captain Searlington. How's it going?"

Madison looked down at the crate full of papers he was holding in front of him. "The usual, I'm either answering phones or jockeying paperwork. Same day, every day for the last ten years."

"You sound like you're regretting not taking that early retirement option brass laid on the table."

Madison shook his head, a bright strip of fire lancing through his eyes. "Not for a second. If I'd have let them push me out, then they would've won. That's what they wanted, my life, my spirit. I'm not happy about sitting out my career behind a desk, but

I'm not going to let the fuckers that did this to me win.

If only Bryan had been strong enough to hold tightly to those convictions. But being a cop, a hands-on cop, being able to be out there in the field meant everything to him.

Bryan nodded his head, that's all he could manage. He smiled politely and made his excuses. He really didn't need to have Madison's attack in his head while he was talking to Justice. He was anxious enough, adding the uneasiness he always felt when in Madison's presence would only add fuel to Justice's fire.

No matter what Justice thought, Bryan wasn't ashamed of him. But when explaining that to Justice, if all Bryan could do was project his sadness for Madison's situation, then he didn't stand much of a chance in changing his husband's mind.

Bryan had just enough time to give himself a mental shake before Justice was filling the doorway to his office.

"Thanks for seeing me."

"Anytime, Jussy. What's going on?"

Justice reached inside of his jacket and pulled out a stack of folded paper. He handed it to Bryan, saying nothing while Bryan unfolded the papers and began to read.

The tiny bit of hope that was blooming in his chest a few moments ago was slowly hardening, sinking to the bottom of his stomach.

"Son of a bitch. You're serving me with a signed divorce petition?"

"Bryan…" the way Justice called his name seemed fake. It was cold, unfeeling, as if Bryan were no more than a stranger on the street.

"You're doing this in my place of business? You couldn't wait for me to get home so we could discuss this in private?"

Bryan watched a cloud of shame fall over Justice's smooth caramel features and understanding began to dawn.

"You didn't want to discuss this in private. You thought if you served me here I'd be too afraid to have this discussion for fear of outing myself?"

"You do love your job, Bryan," the coldness in his voice sounding so odd coming from lips that had spent time touching the most intimate places on Bryan's body.

It was true, Bryan did love his job, but there was no comparison of which mattered more, NYPD or the man standing in front of him.

"What I love is my husband, and this is bullshit and you know it. This was a low blow, Justice. It didn't have to go down like this."

Bryan re-folded the papers and shoved them in the back pocket of his jeans. He stepped close into Justice's space, almost close enough to kiss him. Bryan stood there, chest pulling in deep, hard breaths as he tried his best to figure out what he was really angry about. Was he mad that Justice actually pulled some bullshit like this at his job, or was Bryan furious they were standing this close in his office instead of their home? At home Bryan could do something about the jerking dick in his pants that was threatening to make its presence known. Standing in the middle of his precinct, his options were limited.

"This isn't over," Bryan's hissed words drawing no reaction from the well-trained Marine standing rock-still in his presence.

He gripped hard fingers around the front of Justice's neck and pulled Justice to his lips. Their flesh came together in a fiery clash as Bryan moved angry lips over his husband's mouth.

When Bryan ripped his lips away, he could see Justice trying to piece his unbothered façade back together again.

Bryan rolled his eyes, too pissed to try to get beyond Justice's practiced stoicism. Bryan simply pushed past his rugged form and exited the office.

As he made it to his car he was distracted from his anger by the vibrating of his phone. He looked down to see a text from his sister-in-law, True.

> *Meet me at your place. We need to talk.*

Bryan smacked his hand at his steering wheel. Apparently, this was the fucking day that just kept on giving.

***

Bryan opened the door to True. Her face was impassive, not giving away any of her thoughts.

Damn these Amare children and their ability to wipe emotions from their faces, their bodies, whenever they needed to.

"What can I do for you, True?"

There was no need in presenting platitudes and niceties. This shit, whatever fucked up reason True was standing in his apartment, needed to be over now. His husband signed fucking divorce papers and handed those motherfuckers to him. He did not have time to entertain bullshit, not when he needed to think up a way to save his marriage.

Shit just got real.

"Law called me, told me to help you get our brother to give you another chance."

"And?" He figured she was here to tell him exactly what she wanted him to know. True didn't bite her tongue, so asking her a bunch of questions was pretty much unnecessary. She was going to tell you what she wanted, how she wanted it, and there wasn't much you could do about it.

"You've been fucking over my brother for the last five years. You broke his heart when you left him. All of his hopes and dreams were shattered when you asked to separate. So now because you took a bullet to the chest and found Jesus, Allah,

Buddha, whomever in that coma of yours, I'm supposed to set my brother up for heartache again?"

Her arms were folded over her chest; her legs spread shoulder-width apart. She meant every fucking thing she was saying at this moment.

"Why should I?"

There was only one way he knew how to answer her question. She was right. Bryan had broken Justice's heart when he pushed Jussy away. She was also right that he'd had a crazy emotional experience while he was comatose. But True's ability to correctly read him didn't change one simple fact.

"Because I love him and he loves me."

Bryan's answer wasn't intended to be a get-out-of-jail-free card. He fully accepted his responsibility in making this mess they were all currently muddling through. It weighed on him heavily every waking moment of each day.

"And that's supposed to explain everything? You gotta come better than that bullshit you're slinging right now."

"True, my fucking husband just came to my office to serve me a signed divorce petition. Right now, I don't really give a flying fuck what you think. I've got to find a way to stop Justice from making the biggest fucking mistake of our lives. Do I want your help? Not particularly, because I know you're crazy, and I'm probably going to end up in some fucked up situation messing around with you. But am I desperate enough to let you get involved? Absolutely! At this point, I'd do just about anything to keep my man with me, where he belongs."

A slow smile crawled up her lips and bloomed across her face. "If you're willing to talk to me like that, knowing there are a hundred different ways I can kill you from here, without even laying my hands on you, you must really be willing to do just about anything to get back with my little-big brother."

She stepped closer into his space, her hands in her pockets, her eyes locked on his. "I'm going to help you Bryan, because I know you really do love Justice. But understand this, fuck with my brother's heart again and I will end you. I could give a damn about that badge of yours. With the type of dirt I deal in, they'd never find a body. Understand me, Lieutenant?"

Bryan swallowed carefully. True was intense on her best day, scary on most others. He knew she wasn't just lobbing idle threats at him. She meant that shit with a passion.

"Understood, Dr. Amare."

She nodded her head and slapped a friendly hand on his shoulder. "Let's sit down and talk strategy, Bryan. It's time to get your man back."

Chapter 7

"I don't know about this True," Bryan huffed as he took a seat on the workout bench. "Justice isn't stupid. He's going to walk in here and see right through this bullshit."

True pressed two fingers against her temple and rubbed in a slow circular motion. "Say it with me now Bryan, 'All. Men. Are. Stupid'," she chimed. "Y'all will always try to apply a logical solution to an illogical situation and wonder why the shit doesn't work. If you listen to me, I promise you in just a few minutes you'll be on your way to getting your man back. Just remember that this is a start to the path you guys need to be going down. I'm just gonna get you the opportunity, you're the one that's got to bring it home."

Bryan opened his mouth to respond when a tall dark haired man entered the room. He was somewhere over 6 feet tall, nearly eye-to-eye with

Bryan. His butterscotch skin covered a solid muscular body that Bryan certainly would've had an interest in exploring if he wasn't so in love with Justice.

"Bryan," True intruded upon his thoughts. "This is the newest member of my OT team over at Trinity, Martin Herrera. Martin, this is my brother-in-law, Bryan Smyth."

Bryan gave his sister-in-law a long glance. "Are you sure this is gonna work, True?"

"It worked for Kenneth and Heart, didn't it?"

He took a moment to think about his captain, who also happened to be a first cousin to the Amares, and her husband, Kenneth. Those two fought like the devil and all of God's angels before they finally settled into happiness. If his memory served him correctly, True sent in one of her partners from Trinity to stir up trouble between them. It was volatile for a while, but in the end Kenneth and Heart were now inseparable.

"So you gonna stand here yapping at me all day long?" she asked. "Or are you going to get to work?"

Bryan threw up his hands. This woman was either going to get him beaten, or worse, killed.

I guess both of those selections are better than divorced.

"So Martin you ever work with an injury like mine?" Bryan asked the man politely standing there pretending the conversation Bryan and True were having wasn't awkward.

"Your sister-in-law tells me you had an injury to the chest with a high-caliber round?"

Bryan nodded, just remembering that hellified day made the healing wound in his chest throb. According to the doctors he was all cleared to get back to the business of being Lieutenant Smyth, but the tissues, nerves, and muscles the bullet pierced ached with the memory of that pain.

"Yes, it was a through-and-through actually. The round was so powerful it went from me and into the abdomen of my superior's husband."

Martin watched him for a moment. Bryan knew he was going to get the pity stare, the one that meant, 'I'm so sorry for your experience'. It seemed to repeat itself again in every person's eyes that learned about his ordeal.

He got that people didn't really understand what to say when they found out a person had been shot, but the, 'I'm so sorry for what happened to you' hook and line was kind of old at this point. Bryan wanted to move beyond it. This training and getting back to his day-to-day was moving beyond it. And True was right, if his man wasn't gonna help him get back to his physical norm, the least this training could do was help him set things right with his husband.

"Damn, you must be a tough son of a bitch," Martin praised. "I know dudes in the Corps that were grazed and it was enough for them to give up their career forever. You really ready to go back to the streets?"

A skeptical smile began to build on Bryan's lips. That was the first time anyone ever acknowledged he was doing his job. The job he loved, a job he had every intention of returning to.

Yeah, this working out with the new trainer thing just might work after all.

"I only know how to be two things in life," Bryan responded, "a Marine and a cop. I gave up being a Marine a long time ago. I'd like to hold onto being a cop for a little bit longer."

"If that's what you want, Lieutenant," Herrera's smile offered just a hint of mischief. "Then I'm just the man to deliver that for you."

***

Justice's lungs burned. Running the repeated circle around Gersh's track on Linden Boulevard since the ass crack of dawn had him drenched in sweat and his body screaming, *What the hell, dude*?

Yeah, his father had state-of-the-art workout equipment in the basement gym to keep them all in tip-top shape. He could have easily completed his morning PT there. Knowing his husband and at least two of his siblings were down there working out sent him straight for the familiar school yard. Yeah, it was the coward's way out, keeping him from facing his husband and his family like the man he claimed he was. But every time he saw Bryan, there was this overwhelming need to go back, and he just couldn't risk giving in to it at this moment.

After all this time, he finally had the strength to take his life back. To stop waiting on the fringes for Bryan to see what they had and how valuable it was. The only problem, even though he knew he couldn't continue as they were, it didn't mean he didn't love the man.

Making the conscious decision to divorce your husband was a bold move, sticking to it took strength Justice wasn't certain he had.

After a quick swig of water, Justice looked at his watch and figured the house should be free and clear of Bryan Smyth, so he decided to return home. Less than ten minutes in his car and he was parking in front of his father's house, preparing himself to hide in his bedroom for the rest of the day.

Justice heard voices the moment he opened the door. He looked around him trying to find the direction from which they were coming. This far away he couldn't tell if they were male or female, but he could tell there was more than one.

Logic told him there was a pretty good chance one of those voices belonged to Bryan. If he didn't want to see Bryan taking himself up those stairs was his best bet. Without warning his feet began to move in the direction of the basement door, apparently being smart wasn't on his agenda today.

He walked down the steps and into the basement. The closer he got to the voices the more certain he was one of them was definitely Bryan. The other he couldn't make out. Curiosity peppered with a little bit of concern propelled Justice forward until he was standing at the doorway of the gym watching a tall muscular man rub his fucking hands all over Bryan's back. The last logical thought he had was 'There's probably a very reasonable explanation for this'. But once the blood began boiling in his head, it short-circuited his ability to think in a straight line.

"The hell is going on here?"

Both men looked toward the door in surprise, but neither in a hurry to move from the positions they were holding.

"Oh, you're back?" Bryan's questioning voice sounding a tad bit too blasé for Justice's taste. "True was sure you weren't going to be back for another few hours. This is Martin Herrera, he's gonna be helping me with my training until he goes back to LA with True."

Justice found himself filling the doorway tightening all of his muscles to make certain his chest was broad and big and visible to the fit man currently touching his husband.

"You work with my sister?"

The man nodded, "Yeah, we've worked together a few times over the years. She's taking me on at her rehab center in California. Told me this was sort of an audition for that job."

"Well we won't keep you, Justice," Bryan's interruption pissing Justice off just as much as the idea of Herrera putting his hands back on Bryan's body. "I was just starting to get a little tight so Martin suggested a little bit of a rubdown to loosen me up before my next set. I guess we'll get back to it and catch-up with you later."

Did he just dismiss me?

The answer to Justice's internal thought evident when Bryan turned away from the direction of the door, closed his eyes, and continued to let the stranger grope him. He made a quick turn back toward the stairs. Climbing them two at a time, he was past the first floor landing and on his way to the upstairs apartment.

The need to physically mangle something sat in the middle of his chest. He slammed his father's apartment door behind him, only getting minor relief from the action and the resulting crack of noise through the air.

"You break it, you buy it," a firm voice called from the living room.

"Pops, you're back?" The sound of his father's voice gave Justice's mood a slight lift, until he realized he was going to have to explain why his mood was so foul.

"Well, since my name is on the deed, it shouldn't be all that surprising to find me in my house. What's got you so worked up, little man?"

Even in his anger, no annoyance, no—whatever the hell he was feeling right now—his father's insistence on calling him that nick name made Justice laugh. Considering he had his father by at least two inches in height and thirty pounds in muscle, it was comical his father still referred to him as little anything.

"True is using Bryan as a test-case for her new hire. I mean, she knows how serious it is for Bryan to be up to snuff when he goes back to work. Why the hell would she put a newbie on the job? If he fucks up this last leg of Bryan's rehab I'm coming straight for her."

"You know I'm a problem solver, brother. So if you've got one, bring it," True said from behind him.

"That supposed to be a threat, True?" Justice kept his eyes on his father as his senses clocked his sister's movements into the room from behind him. "You might walk around big and bad with the rest of the world, but ain't nobody in here shook by you."

She was standing beside Justice now, a smile curving slowly on her lips. She walked past him, not really acknowledging his presence—other than her smile—as she stretched to place a sweet kiss on their father's cheek.

"Glad you're home, Pops." She moved beyond the middle of the living room floor and sat down casually on the couch facing both men. She crossed her legs with ease, then removed a combat blade from her boot. As soon as her fingers surrounded the hilt, she casually ran the blade across the fingernails of her opposite hand, as if it were no more than an enlarged nail file.

She looked up, her gaze locking with Justice's. "Fear is the mind's way of telling you when something can harm you. If you're too stupid to figure that out, then I pity you. I'm here anytime you want to do anything more than talk little-big brother."

Justice pressed a half-step forward before he felt his father's palm against his chest. "You, stand down," he commanded Justice in his General Hunter Amare voice. When he heard True snicker, he pointed his finger at her, "And you, stop baiting your brother."

She rolled her eyes, and shrugged her shoulders. She always was the most disrespectful of all of his siblings, but even she knew to chill the fuck out when their father used his commanding officer voice.

"True," their father continued. "What's this I hear about you hiring some newbie to work with Bryan?"

"Pops, Jussy is just being dramatic. There's nothing new about Herrera. He's worked in combat rehab for nearly twenty years. It's been his job to get Marines and sailors back to their combat-ready condition and back on the field. He just retired, and I snatched him up for Trinity. Since he's in town, I asked him to come work with Bryan."

Their father turned his questioning glare at Justice. "Why aren't you training Bryan?"

"Finally, someone in this room is asking the right question," True offered.

"Shut up, True," Justice countered.

A quick clap to the side of his head brought Justice's focus back to his father. "What are you, thirteen?" The gruff sound of his father's voice felt like a tug on a leash around Justice's neck. "Don't talk to your sister like that. Answer me. Why the hell aren't you training your husband? Especially since you've been given leave from the Corps to do so?"

Justice imagined most sons would agree there was nothing like being dressed down by your father. But when your father was a career military man, there was an extra special twist to a father's ability to verbally chastise his son.

Some of his bluster seeped into the air on a long sigh as Justice felt his chest deflate. "I decided to proceed with the divorce. Considering that, I didn't think it best for me to work with Bryan."

"True, give your brother and me some privacy."

Without question or comment, True stood and exited the room. She, like Justice, understood their father's verbal cues. General Amare was not happy.

"Pops—"

"I don't want to hear any excuses, Justice. Reasons, that's all I want."

Justice nodded his head and took True's vacated seat on the couch. His father grabbed the high-backed chair sitting in the corner and placed it directly in front of where Justice sat.

"Pops, I know how much you love Bryan, how much you all love Bryan. But I can't do this anymore."

"Do what, honor your promise before God and man to love and cherish him?"

"Pops, it's not as simple as that. I'm just giving Bryan what he's been asking for all these years. I'm setting him free."

"Justice…don't do this," the warm concern that wrapped around his father's words did more to rub the tender spot inside of his heart raw than provide comfort. His father, his siblings, they all spoke to him as if he didn't know what he was doing, as if he couldn't recognize what he was losing by walking away from the man he loved.

It hurt. It hurt worse than any wound he'd ever received in the middle of battle. Unfortunately life had proven to him that just because something hurt, didn't mean it wasn't the right thing to do.

"Well then, if you're determined to follow this course, understand this," his father cautioned, "if you throw something away, you have no say in what happens to it once it hits the bottom of the trash can. It is no longer yours. Since you've decided to end your marriage, you've decided that means you can't help in Bryan's recovery. All of that is fine. But that also means you don't get a say in any of the decisions surrounding his recovery, including who his trainer happens to be or what methods he chooses to employ to help Bryan heal. Stay out of your sister's way."

"Pops—"

"That was an order, Colonel Amare." The General's voice was strong and certain, enforcing the message that he meant what he said.

Justice stood, his back ramrod straight, his fingers pointed in salute at his head, his eyes locked on a target behind his father against the wall. "Yes sir, General Amare."

"Dismissed."

Justice swallowed the hard ball of anger in his throat. If there weren't twenty-one years of military discipline in his past he might have let the frustration singeing his tongue slip out. Too entrenched in military life, Justice nodded and made a quick exit from the living room. His father had laid down the law, and Justice had no choice but to listen. Then why was his anger swelling inside of him? His father hadn't fought him on the divorce, not as much as Justice anticipated he would have. Then why was Justice so bothered by his father's edict, to keep his nose out of Bryan's rehab…his life?

The answer was there, but Justice refused to sweep away the emotional debris cluttering his mind as he walked out of the apartment, down the stairs and out of his family home. Searching for that answer might keep him from doing what he'd already set his mind to do, the right thing. He was Justice, and Justice always did what was right, even when it felt so wrong.

***

"I hope you know what you're doing, True." Hunter Amare spoke into the air as he watched his son exit their home.

"Don't I always?" True's voice crept from the shadows as she re-entered the room.

Hunter knew she was right; her instinct to handle most tactical situations was innate. But this wasn't some faceless enemy on the battlefield. This wasn't a demonized villain one could feel vindicated in conquering. This was his youngest son, her brother, and Bryan. If she got this wrong, Hunter wasn't certain if their family would endure the fall out.

"If we're to survive this, like never before you'd better be correct, True," the weariness and concern he felt filling his heart bled into his voice.

"I know what's at stake, Pops." True moved closer until she was standing directly in front of Hunter. "I know what it feels like to lose the one you love. I promise I'll do everything I can to keep Justice from knowing that pain too."

Hunter acknowledged her decree with the slightest nod of his head. He didn't know the specifics, but he'd recognized the weight of loss on her shoulders a long time ago. True was his youngest, but she believed it was her duty to protect her brothers. He had every confidence his daughter would wage war to guard Justice's happiness. Because that's what family did.

The Amares were each other's greatest strength, the sum always stronger than the individual parts. Their enemies cowered throughout the world at their might and prowess. The secret to their strategic success was simple; their bond was their fiercest weapon, their love, their greatest asset.

He was their leader, both in war and in blood. His responsibility as such wasn't just to win, but to recognize when the win wasn't worth the threat to his team, his family. Putting his trust in True wasn't just an act of faith where her abilities were concerned, it was equally a test in how much he trusted his own judgment as well.

Chapter 8

Justice ran alongside his newest set of *poolees*. These poor kids, newly signed to the Marine Corps, but not yet sworn in, were getting a lesson in abuse as Justice ran them through several paces. Yeah, this was about conditioning them for basic training, but it was more about Justice needing to burn his jealousy out of his system so he could think of something other than another man's hands on his husband.

When he was finished torturing them, he left the track and headed back to his house for a shower and hopefully an attitude adjustment.

The absence of his father's big caddy sitting in front of the house was a relief. He didn't see any of his siblings' vehicles either.

"Good, not up for anyone's bullshit."

He ran up the stairs, pulling his drenched sweatshirt over his head as he walked into the apartment.

A quick unanswered, 'Pops, you home?' let him know his bad mood wasn't going to be interrupted. Leaving a trail of dirty workout clothes on the floor, he headed for the bathroom, where he adjusted the shower spray to as hot as he could bear it.

The moment water met skin, relief began to bleed through him and his anger loosened its grip on him. He was beginning to relax until his mind brought forth the image of Bryan laying down shirtless on the massage table, skin brown and buttery, muscles tight and sculpted and the brief relief he'd been working on left him.

Somehow in his muddled mind, Herrera's hands became his own and the familiar sensation of his fingertips meeting Bryan's skin overtook his senses. He pressed his palms against the cool tile of the shower, hoping to disrupt the sense memory his mind was replaying. No such luck. He could still feel hot, supple skin beneath his fingers.

Familiar tingling in his balls brought his cock's attention to the imaginary party going on in his head.

Being the traitorous bastard that it was, his dick didn't seem to care that none of the images playing behind Justice's eyes hadn't actually happened. Apparently it was down for the ride anyway.

In his vision, Bryan turned over, looking at Justice with a sexy smile. Bryan cupped a handful of Justice's bulge, giving it a hearty squeeze.

"Fuck," Justice muttered, as the sensation of actual touch brought him slightly out of his daydream to realize it was his own hand on his leaking cock. He looked down at his straining flesh pulsing in his hand. The single eye seemingly staring up at him, winking, begging him to finish what his imagination had started.

"Fuck it," he relented, grabbing the bottle of shower gel and squeezing way too much in his palm. He spread his legs, placed an anchoring palm against the wall, and wrapped firm fingers around his cock. That first stroke was so fucking sweet his knees almost gave out beneath him. Taking a moment to recover his stance, he stroked himself again.

He lost himself in the sensitive slide of his palm against aching flesh. Flashes of tender brown skin permeated his mind, urging his movements, pressing him toward completion. A few more quick and hard strokes and Justice felt fire traveling quickly from his heavy sack, rushing down the length of his pulsing cock. That first spurt of cum brought sincere bliss as it ripped through him and landed in a loud splat against the wall. His fist kept pumping, oblivious to the demands of his sensitive head to stop, until his balls were drained and he was plastered against the wall, breathless, boneless, and in need of support.

Slowly his brain cells began to work again, rerouting his blood flow to its normal and needed pattern. Only one thought pushed past the post-orgasm fog in his head. If the thought of Bryan's touch could render Justice so completely ruined, how the fuck was he going to last the remainder of his life without ever experiencing it again?

***

"Almost there, Bryan." The boom of Martin's voice filled the room with excitement. "Come on. You can do it, man. Give it to me."

Every muscle in Bryan's body was taut and burning with fatigue. Every ounce of his strength being depleted as he fought to keep up this grueling pace. The residual ache was so sweet, both a deterrent and an enticement to keep pushing, to meet that just-out-of-reach prize.

"Fuck, Martin…come on," Bryan bit out through clenched teeth.

"Almost there, Bryan! I promise…so close."

Bryan kept pushing, the motion instinctual, thinking about it would yield an inevitable conclusion. He wanted to last…for Martin, for himself.

"Yes," Martin howled. "That's it, right there; you've got it, Bryan. It's all you, this is yours."

Bryan gave one final push of the barbell above his chest upward until he felt the weight in his palms dissipating as Martin pulled it back onto the rack.

"Damn man," Martin smiled as he cheered, celebrating Bryan's completion of the new workout regimen he'd created for him. This was their third program in as many months and every time Martin set new goals for Bryan, he did his best to smash through them. "You are killing it lately. Bench pressing all that weight and we've only been at this new routine for a couple of weeks? If you're doing that after an injury, I can't even imagine what you were like before you were hurt."

Bryan shook out the prickling nerves in his shaky arms. Before the shooting he was able to press more than his own body weight. With Martin's help, it appeared he'd be back to his norm sooner than he'd believed possible.

"Thanks man, you've been a life saver." It was true, Bryan needed to be in the best shape possible to return to the NYPD. Heart was already giving him hell about when he was returning. Yeah, there were others that filled in as her second during his absence, but according to his captain, 'Ain't none of them motherfuckers you. Hurry up and get your ass back. '

She wasn't harassing him, wasn't threatening his job, just trying to express how much she needed him at her side. It was as good of a 'miss you' as he was going to get from that one.

"Don't thank me," Martin responded. "This is all you, my friend. Come lie down on the table. Let me loosen up your chest before we get out of here today."

Bryan headed for the table, stretching out slowly, relaxing his back on the cushioned surface. As soon as Martin's fingers pressed into his flesh, Bryan's eyes closed, falling willingly into the easy repose the deep tissue stimulation lulled him into.

"Any plans this weekend?" Martin's voice sounded distant, as if he were speaking to Bryan from a great distance. Bryan focused on his voice again, attempting to remain conscious enough to carry on the conversation.

"Nah, just gonna hang in my apartment."

"Isn't that what you did last weekend?" Martin's fingers continued to press into Bryan's flesh, keeping him from tensing up again.

Bryan blew out a long breath. He knew exactly how pitiful his life was, he was living it. Martin's reminder that Bryan didn't have shit going on in his life since Justice decided their marriage wasn't worth fighting for chilled him from the inside.

Justice had maintained radio silence since he'd demanded a divorce. He'd come by their apartment once or twice a week to check on Bryan's progress, but he spent most of his time at his familial home.

Every time he laid eyes on Justice, Bryan wanted to beg him for another chance. But his sister-in-law told him not to. It went against everything inside of him, but he held back and listened to True anyway. Why? Leaning to his own understanding is what landed him in the fuck-awful place he and Justice were currently residing in. At this point anyone else's advice had to be better than wallowing in this pit of love hell.

"Come on man, you can't just work yourself like crazy in here with me, and then hide in your house all weekend, every weekend. Why aren't you getting out more?"

Bryan turned Martin's question over in his head. The answer was simple. He didn't want to be anywhere without his husband.

"I'm going through a divorce right now. It hasn't put me in the best of moods."

"Listen, I've been there man. I know what it's like to be in the middle of losing the one you love. If you keep sitting locked up in the apartment you're gonna wind up eating your gun after a while. There's a new action flick playing at Linden, we can go there, then walk down the block for a couple of beers at the diner."

His self-imposed solitude probably wasn't the best thing for him right now. No, he wasn't at the point where the despair was so bad he felt suicide was the only way out, but who knew what dark places his mind would travel to if he didn't switch things up sooner or later.

Still, this just didn't feel right. His solitude was a blessing right now, he wasn't ready to step outside and deal with the rest of the world while he grieved.

Bryan opened his eyes to meet the compassionate stare Martin offered him. He placed a hand over Martin's, stilling it from its kneading motion.

"Martin, I—"

"I'm certain this isn't what the medical community would consider an appropriate way to anticipate and execute your patient's needs."

Bryan looked up at Martin and realized Martin hadn't been the one to speak. He turned his head to the doorway to find Justice walking into the room. He sat up, swinging his legs over the side of the table but still remaining seated on the table.

"I'm sure there's a meaning somewhere in there, but I didn't catch it, Mr. Amare," Martin responded with a practiced patience Bryan was certain had to come from years of being a healthcare professional.

"That's Colonel Amare," Justice's rough growl resonated throughout the room without courtesy or preamble. "And since you seem to have a problem comprehending, let me make it plain for you. Is it standard practice for you to try seduction as a means of therapy? Every time I see you, your hands are all over my husband. Now I come in and you're in the middle of asking him on a date."

Bryan's head snapped back at that one.

Wait, when the hell did I get asked on a date? Where was I when that shit happened?

"Justice, you're completely misunderstanding this," Bryan interrupted.

"Bryan, I didn't misunderstand shit," Justice countered.

"Justice, Martin and I—"

"Bryan, as far as I understand it, the two of you are getting a divorce. You don't really owe him an explanation about anything," Martin offered.

Hands fisted at his side, nostrils flaring, Justice took a step forward. Bryan hopped off the table and stood in front of his husband, blocking his path to Martin.

"You know like I know…you'd mind your damn business when it came to me and mine," Justice's anger was on boil, threatening to tip over and spill out of every orifice or pore he possessed.

"Is he yours? Last I'd heard you threw him away."

Justice pressed forward again and Bryan had to land solid hands flat against his chest to keep him from advancing.

"Enough. The two of you cut it out now," Bryan interrupted as he looked over his shoulder to Martin. "Please excuse us for just a moment. I'll be out in a minute."

Martin took a moment to assess the situation before he nodded and made his way through the door.

"What the hell is your problem?" Bryan rounded on him in a quick, aggressive turn. "You come in here lobbing accusations at both Martin and me? What the fuck is wrong with you?"

"Bryan, that man is not worried about your training. He's worried about getting a piece of your ass."

Bryan ran a harsh hand over his short cropped hair. "No, he's not. He's actually been pretty awesome at helping me get back to baseline. He's certainly done more than you have at this point."

"Bryan," Justice sighed his name. The sound reverent, like a whispered prayer on his husband's lips was always enough to still the storms of life inside of him. But tonight, it just pissed Bryan off.

"Don't come in here with that, Justice. To date you haven't done dick to help me get back to where I was before that bullet entered my chest. Martin has.

If letting him fuck me is the price I have to pay for him doing that, then that is my decision and mine alone to make. You don't get to say shit about it. You wanted a divorce, now deal with all that comes with it," Bryan's annoyance rattled through his bones, surprising even him at just how aggravated he was with Justice. "Including the knowledge that after twenty-one years together, that I'll be taking another man to my bed."

Bryan pushed past Justice and headed for the door. That beer Martin offered was sounding pretty good right about now.

Chapter 9

Bryan sat at the bar, letting the burn of the whiskey shot he'd just swallowed spread through him. After his fight with Justice, Martin suggested they get a drink first before they sat through the movie.

"You all right, man?'

Bryan blinked a few times to bring Martin into focus, hoping clearer vision would somehow improve his hearing.

"I will be as soon as I get another one of these in me,' he responded as he dangled the empty shot glass between his fingers.

"I'm sorry I caused that dust up back there." A palpable blanket of remorse rested on Martin's shoulders. The way he was slumped over the bar's edge and slowly drinking his whiskey painted a sorrowful picture.

Bryan waved his hand. "Wasn't your fault my soon-to-be ex is an asshole. He thinks you're just trying to fuck me. Was he right? Are you just looking for a quick fuck? If you are, you should know I'm not the best candidate for that sort of thing right now."

Martin laughed a bit before shaking his head. "I wasn't hitting on you, Bryan.

Bryan lifted a brow in surprise. "Then why did you agree to True's plan?"

"Because she's a good friend of mine and because anyone looking at you and Justice can see how much love there is between you. If someone had done something like this for me, maybe my wife and I might still be together."

"So you're really cool with being in the middle of my dramatic gay love story?"

"Dramatic, a little, but as for the gay part, I don't think these kinds of emotions are only present in a gay relationship."

"That's mighty enlightened of you." Bryan cocked his head as he watched his companion. Herrera's thoughtful eyes screamed of sincerity, as if coaxing Bryan to trust him. If only more people in the world understood that love was love, and it didn't really matter who was doing the loving.

"I don't know about enlightened. I just know after spending the last twenty years of my life seeing how war breaks people psychologically and physically, I know there's a lot more shit in the world to worry about, to get upset about, than who you're fucking."

Bryan nodded his agreement. Too bad the rest of the world couldn't or wouldn't see it that way.

"Can I ask you a question?" With a nod from Bryan, Martin continued. "What led you here, to this place where your husband is asking you for a divorce?"

"A lot of bad shit that neither of us could have anticipated when we married," Bryan answered. "I don't come from the most progressive family. I grew up in a small conservative town in the South where most share the same mindset. In their eyes, who I am, who I love is wrong."

"But you got out, found Justice?" Martin asked.

"Barely," Bryan replied. "My parents discovered I was gay when they walked in on my seventeen-year-old self getting his first blow job. My father beat me until I passed out. The next day he shipped me off to the Marines. That's where I met Justice."

"It wasn't easy, but I learned—with Justice's help—that there's nothing wrong with who and what I am."

Martin watched him carefully, nodding his head, hedging him to continue on with his explanation.

"It took a long time for me to learn to love who I am. But the problem is, I'm not out at work. My boss knows because she happens to be related to my husband. But the rest of the department has no idea. When I was shot and Justice had to be there making the decisions, it put him in a very tough spot of trying to take care of me, while maintaining my secret."

"After all that, you don't think your fellow cops know?" Martin's question was valid. It was something he would have been concerned about himself if it weren't for Heart.

"My captain is my rock. She hand-picked the officers who investigated my shooting, as well as the ones that guarded my door. They were all sympathizers or members of my community that would guard my privacy as well as they did their own."

The bartender handed them their second round of drinks. After a brief clinking of glasses, the two men downed the shots and continued their conversation.

"That whole ordeal wore on Justice more than I understood. It was his breaking point."

"Yeah, but that doesn't seem like enough to end a nearly two-decade relationship. What really happened, I mean before your shooting?"

Bryan slumped against the bar. He'd only known this man for a short time and already he was calling Bryan's bullshit. A chill settled in Bryan's bones. The lock he kept fixed to the door of these memories never turned at all if Bryan could help it. Remembering always made the hurt surface. Five years and he still wasn't over it like everyone believed he should be.

"We lost our daughter in-utero. Some strange recessive trait I passed off to her," Bryan murmured by way of explanation. "One day we were happy, expectant fathers. The next, she was gone."

Martin was quiet for a moment. From the corner of his eye, Bryan could see his bar-mate lift his hand to the bartender and hold up two fingers.

"I don't even have words for that. Losing a kid is something that can shake the strongest of couples."

"It didn't just shake us, it hurt us. What decimated us was my guilt. I couldn't get beyond it, still having a hard time. It ate at us, poisoned my decision-making process until the only solution I could come up with to fix things was to leave my husband. We've been struggling back and forth for the last five years attempting to put ourselves back together. All this time it's been Jussy trying to patch us up, but after seeing the song and dance my life has become, I guess he figured it just wasn't worth loving me any longer."

Martin placed a friendly hand on Bryan's shoulder. "I don't know your man very well, but if he possesses even half the smarts his sister does, he knows how lucky he is to have loved you. If he could've gotten his hands on me tonight, I might not be drinking my liquor so well. He was only that mad because he cares. All isn't lost just yet."

The bartender sat their third round in front of them. Martin picked them up, carefully handing one to Bryan.

"Let's finish this, we've got to get back to the theatre to get good seats," Martin offered.

They clinked their glasses again and swallowed their liquor in one synchronous gulp. Bryan still didn't feel great, but Martin's words had given him just enough hope to not lose himself completely in what remained of the fifth of whiskey shelved behind the bar. That had to be a win, right?

Chapter 10

As soon as he heard the lock turn from the outside, Justice was on his feet and heading in the direction of the door.

"It's two o' clock in the fucking morning and you're just dragging your ass in here now?"

Justice watched glass-like eyes squint as they attempted to focus on him. He pulled Bryan by his collar, bringing him close enough to soak up the intoxicating scent of Bryan's natural man-spice aroma mixed with liquor.

"You went drinking with him?"

Bryan's eyes focused on him a split second before he pulled out of Justice's grasp. "Yeah, we had a few then went to see a movie. What of it?"

"You drove in your condition?"

"Nearly dying makes you a little gun-shy about doing shit that can kill you. Linden is around the corner. I parked my car before we hit the bar and I walked home. Herrera took a cab." Bryan pushed past him and headed for the bathroom. He opened his pants and pulled out his long cock before positioning himself in front of the toilet.

"A little privacy?" Bryan quipped.

"Not anything I haven't seen before." Justice wedged his shoulder against the doorframe as he watched Bryan. He had to admit, watching Bryan take a piss wasn't on his 'Things that turn me on list', but he wasn't about to give Bryan an inch of privacy until he knew every fucking detail of the evening Bryan spent with that bastard Herrera.

Bryan shrugged his shoulders, oblivious to or unconcerned with Justice's building anger, and relieved himself without further thought. When he was done, he washed his hands then turned the shower on and adjusted the spray.

As he began to remove his clothing he stopped to look at Justice. "I've had a long day. I'm gonna take a shower and take my ass to bed. You wanna fight? You'll be fighting alone tonight."

Without giving Justice another glance or thought, Bryan stepped inside of the darkened shower stall.

Justice stood in the middle of the floor waiting, for what he couldn't really pinpoint. Acknowledgement, an explanation, contrition, or something from Bryan that expressed some form of regret that he'd done something to piss Justice off. Instead, Bryan's slightly drunk ass—if his whistling of some pop tune was any indication of his intoxication level—continued on behind the smoky shower glass as if Justice weren't even in the room.

Bryan finished his shower, pulled a towel from the nearby rack and tied it around his waist. He stepped around Justice, and headed for their bedroom. Justice tried hard not to stare at Bryan's water-slicked skin. Bryan at any given time was a turn-on for him. Bryan naked and wet, looking like something Justice should be licking or sopping up with a biscuit, had a way of making him forget his train of thought.

Justice knew he was supposed to be mad about something. Watching his man saunter in front of him, shoulders pulled back in confidence, the globes of his ass sitting high and tight, what a vision. Justice could scarcely remember what he'd eaten for dinner, let alone the complicated trigger to his inner-asshole.

He palmed the hard bulge of his jean-clad cock and closed his eyes, trying his damnedest to remain focused on anything other than being buried in Bryan's ass. After a few moments of fighting with his mind and body, he walked into their bedroom. Bryan was still in his towel, sitting at the edge of the foot of the bed.

"Bryan, I can't believe you're really going to let this asshole fuck with your recovery like this. You fucking know better. All this jack-off is after is getting a piece of ass."

"So what if he is?" Bryan's response striking a fast and fierce blow to Justice's heart. "So what if the only thing he wants from me is a good, hard fuck? Why the fuck does that matter to you? Why do you get a say in that? You just filed divorce papers. Obviously you don't care about who fucks me or who I fuck."

Molten heat carved through the walls of his chest, into the center of his heart. The gripping pain caused his breath to rush past his lips.

"I will always care about you, Bryan. About everything you do," he whispered.

Bryan's flat palms rested against his spread thighs, holding his heavy shoulders up as they threatened to slump in defeat.

"You don't act like it. You act like you don't want anything to do with me. Like you hate me." Bryan flinched as he spoke. As if the thought of Justice hating him physically hurt.

Justice averted his eyes. He knew if he found the same sadness in Bryan's eyes as he heard in his words, he was going to crumble right where he stood.

"I've never lived in the closet, Bryan. I've been out since I knew what gay meant. I married you knowing that you weren't comfortable with your sexuality. That was my fault. I shouldn't have fought you over the divorce when you asked me for it. I should have seen the writing on the wall then. I loved you so much. I couldn't bear to think of walking away."

"And now you can?" Bryan's words were quiet, but the question shook him from the inside out making Justice's body twitch with nervous energy.

No.

The small word bounced off the inside of his head and made its way to his hollow heart. This was killing him. Letting go of the only man he'd loved, relinquishing his claim on Bryan, was breaking him.

"What happened while I was in that coma to make you give up on us, Justice? Why are you so hell-bent on giving up now?" The mixture of frustration and pain in Bryan's voice was nearly choking Justice. "For five fucking years I pushed to end our marriage and you refused. You fought for us, even when I couldn't. And now that I can finally see what a fool I was you want to bounce? What made this happen, Justice?"

"I just got tired of being the only one fighting for us. After watching you nearly die, I didn't have the energy to come back to us fighting about these same issues. Your fear to live in the light as a gay man has been slowly killing us for years," Justice offered. "I'm just finally giving you the freedom to live as you've always wanted, in the shadows."

Justice heard an audible breath cross Bryan's lips. Its heavy sound pulling his gaze from their current position on the floor to his husband's face.

He expected to find the sadness he'd been avoiding, but instead he found Bryan's features twisted into an angry scowl.

"You know what Justice…fuck you.'

Chapter 11

Bryan brushed past Justice and pulled out a pair of boxer briefs from his drawer. Arguing while naked with his dick swinging freely wasn't going to help him win this debate, so he quickly pulled them on and threw the now-damp towel on the nearby weight bench.

"You don't know shit about why I asked for the separation," Bryan continued.

"I know before you got on the phone with your hateful mother, we were grieving the fresh loss of our daughter together. Five minutes after a phone conversation with her and you were telling me you wanted to separate.

"She told you God was punishing you for attempting to bring a child into our supposed sin and your response to that bullshit was to leave me. What else am I supposed to assume? You left because she shamed you into believing we were wrong for loving each other."

Bryan didn't need a reminder of that conversation. His mother's hateful words made her as cold and dead as their daughter was as far as Bryan was concerned.

That one conversation had cost Bryan everything: the love of his husband, the right to grieve their daughter, and the hope that one day his family would be able to evolve beyond their hate and love him for who he really was.

All of it was gone. Broken. Destroyed.

"It didn't have anything to do with being ashamed of us, Justice. I was never ashamed to be your husband," Bryan growled, attempting to keep his anger in check. He pulled his wallet off of the dresser and slapped it against Justice's chest. "Would a man who was ashamed of you do this? No, I don't walk around with a rainbow flag stamped across my forehead, but that doesn't mean that I cower in shame about my sexuality or the man I love either."

***

Bryan moved quickly, the fitted cotton of his boxer briefs laying low on his hips briefly distracting Justice from the conversation they were in the middle of. Maybe he should have thought better of picking this fight while his man was naked save for the slight piece of material covering his nudity.

Once he refocused on their conversation, Justice slowly opened the wallet and looked down at his husband's driver's license. The picture was familiar, the same one he remembered Bryan taking all those years ago when he'd moved to New York after he left the Marines. The only difference between this and the original was the name, Bryan Amare.

"When did you change your name? Why would you change it? I asked you to carry my name before we married and you said no, said it would be too much of a hassle to change all of your documents over."

Bryan kept his hands fixed on his hips, making the broad expanse of his chest tighten as the muscles beneath moved. It might've been a mark of his frustration, but the only purpose it was serving for Justice was stoking his desire for the man.

"I changed my name almost as soon as we got married. I just never changed it at the department. By the time I was ready, you and I were going through so much shit that I didn't think you'd want me to carry your name. Then I decided that I didn't even care if you did, that loving you had made me just as much an Amare as those of you born into the name. So there," Bryan challenged. "There goes your theory that I ran because I was ashamed of you, of us. Whatcha got now?"

Nothing, he had exactly nothing. Justice stood there in silence as he processed what Bryan was saying to him.

"Then what? What the hell was it all about?" Justice demanded.

Just thinking back on that time hurt. They were in the process of burying their precious daughter. Life seemed like an endless black hole of pain and the only thing Justice had anchoring him was Bryan and their love for one another. He'd reached out to Bryan to pull him up out of the mire and his husband had pulled his hand back and walked away.

After five years of begging Bryan to piece his heart back together, Justice was done. He was finished with this entire scenario. If Bryan couldn't shake off his homophobic family's hold on him, then Justice would walk away and live his life alone and free.

Bryan stood directly in front of him, forcing Justice to meet his gaze.

"I'm gonna do you a favor, Justice. This is the same favor your cousin Heart did for me when I first suggested we take a breather. She stood up, and told me when I was being an unnecessary asshole. I'm going to do that for you now. Don't fuck up a good thing just because you think you're being righteous.

Stop being a self-sacrificing bitch. Man up and fight for your goddamn man. I'm not ashamed of us Justice, I never have been."

"Bryan, you didn't want folks on the job to know who you were. I did not imagine that shit. I didn't imagine you using my cousin as your beard for years in the department."

"I have never told anyone that Heart and I were anything more than friends and colleagues," Bryan answered.

Justice folded his arms across his chest. Yeah, that might have been technically true, but they both knew Bryan hadn't done anything to disabuse people of that notion either. It wasn't until Heart met and married her husband, Kenneth Searlington, that folks realized Bryan and Heart weren't together.

"I have never allowed anyone to believe I was with anyone but you, Bryan," Justice stated. "I don't feel the need to make folks comfortable about my goddamned life."

"You know what, Justice? It's real easy to live freely when you don't have to worry about the reprisal that comes later."

"What the fuck is that supposed to mean? I'm a Marine. You think being gay and serving in the Corps is all about the fun times?" Justice rolled his eyes, his annoyance evident in his posture.

"Your daddy is a four-star General," Bryan added. "You really think folks saw you for who you were and accepted it? They knew fucking with you essentially meant fucking with their careers. I work on the fucking streets. If my fellow cops don't have my fucking back, my life isn't worth shit when I'm out there. I wasn't ashamed of us, Justice; only afraid of the assholes in my department doing me like they did Madison. The risk is too great to my fucking life."

Justice leaned against the dresser for needed support as Bryan's revelation pressed against the center of his chest. Justice worked hard in his career to get to where he was. Making Colonel in the

Marines as an enlisted man in twenty-one years was almost an impossibility. But he'd sacrificed so much and made it happen.

Although he'd worked hard, he wasn't stupid; he knew the fact that he was a General's kid had benefited him. It might not have facilitated his rise in the ranks, but as an out gay man in the military, it definitely helped to keep some of the bigots in their place.

Bryan didn't have that in the NYPD. There was no one there making certain Bryan's ability to succeed on his own merit wasn't fucked with. Other than Heart, Bryan didn't have anyone there to protect his life.

"Then why did you ask for the separation? I know it had something to do with your family. You were different after that conversation with your mother," Justice entreated.

He watched some of the ire seep out of Bryan as he stepped back and returned to his perch at the end of their bed.

"Meeting you saved me, Justice," Bryan's admission both warmed and pained Justice.

Justice remembered what Bryan was like in the early days of their relationship. Hurt, fragile, angry, and convicted, so broken that Justice often worried he'd never be able to love, let alone allow Justice to love him.

"In so many different ways I was snatched from the clutches of death when I fell in love with you, Justice. I was exiled for the great sin of being gay, abandoned by everyone that was supposed to love me. But you found me, loved me, and then brought me to a family that would love me.

"You gave me everything, Justice. Everything I ever wanted was part of my reality because you loved me and graced me with it. Up until the moment we decided to expand our family I had nothing to give you in return. When you said you wanted a baby, I knew I had to be the one to give it to you. It was the only thing that would measure up to how much love you'd blessed me with.

Bryan's voice trembled on that last word. He pulled his eyes away from Justice's for a brief moment, as if looking at Justice wore on the thin veil of control Bryan was gingerly holding on to.

"I knew if I could give you that, I'd be deserving of your love. I'd truly be your partner."

Justice's soul ached at how small Bryan's voice sounded. How long had his husband felt like this, as if he'd had nothing of significance to offer Justice except for a child?

"When she died, it broke me. But it wasn't until my mother said those hateful things to me that I began to believe she was right. God was punishing me, not for being gay, but for being me. He must have hated me; I was so broken, so worthless, that he allowed my blood to be the thing that killed our child, killed us."

"Bryan, you did nothing wrong. It was a recessive trait, a freak of nature; no one could have predicted it. You did all of the genetic counseling, it never showed up in any of the tests you underwent before we began the artificial insemination process. You couldn't have blamed yourself for this all this time?"

But he was, and apparently he had. His slumped shoulders and bowed head were proof of his burden. Bryan was a man in pain, a man weighed down by guilt.

"She was the one thing you wanted, and the one thing I couldn't give you. After you'd saved me, I was so fucked up inside I couldn't give you the gift you wanted most. I couldn't keep you in a marriage knowing I couldn't give you the child you'd asked me for."

Justice took the few steps between them and kneeled down between Bryan's legs. He ran a gentle hand over Bryan's cropped, dark curls and let it travel until it met the wet warmth of his tear-dampened cheek.

"You were all I needed, all I wanted. Honor...she..." Justice struggled to speak through the thick pain cutting through him. They hadn't spoken her name since the day they put her in the ground.

Justice remembered the day they'd chosen her name. Bryan insisted they would keep with the Amare tradition of naming their children for the virtues they hoped the child would embrace.

She will be a daughter of Justice, she must be Honor.

The name was perfect and so was she, too perfect for the ugly world they inhabited.

"I didn't want a child, Bryan, I wanted your child. I wanted Honor because she was part of you. She was to be the result of growth in our relationship. Honor was not meant to complete, or bear the weight of our relationship. Her end should not have meant our end. We should have grabbed on to one another when she died, not run to our separate corners. I didn't blame you then, and I don't blame you now."

He wrapped strong arms around Bryan's shaking shoulders and surrounded him in love. It was what

Bryan needed, what he'd always needed. Five years lost because he was too foolish to ask the right questions, and Bryan was too guilty to let Justice help bear the weight of his pain.

He'd been so unwise, so wrapped up in his need to sacrifice himself and his heart that Justice hadn't realized the man he loved was sinking in despair. He'd blamed Bryan for their brokenness, instead of seeing the truth. Bryan was shattered and in need of being pieced back together.

Believing Bryan was ashamed of their love gave Justice the ability to latch on to his moral superiority with both hands. The high ground, it was his favorite place to be. And now sitting here, facing the sickening truth of his ignorance, Justice felt ill.

His man had been suffering and Justice's only concern was being pissed off because he thought Bryan couldn't bear to free himself from his closet. If he'd paid half as much attention to Bryan's heart as he had his anger and indignation, maybe they could've spent these broken years mending their marriage and each other together.

It was too late for maybes. Justice wouldn't allow another moment to be lost to uncertainty. Bryan needed him. If it was the only thing he ever did, Justice would be there for his husband, make this right.

Five years lost to Justice's arrogance. The only thing he had to show for it was useless pain. And the truth was he deserved that.

Chapter 12

Justice leaned in and chased Bryan's tears with warm kisses.

"I failed you, I failed her," Bryan's words were so faint Justice could barely make them out.

"You loved us." Justice pressed firm lips against Bryan's mouth. "That's all either of us ever required of you."

Justice traced strong fingers along the line of Bryan's jaw, down his neck, across his shoulders and down to his chest where the healed scar marked the exit of a near-fatal bullet. If things had gone differently, he might have lost Bryan that day, might have never had the opportunity to know how haunted his husband had really been.

"I'm sorry for not seeing all of your pain, Bryan, for not understanding how much you really needed me. I promise I will never let you down like that again."

Justice meant those words, needed Bryan to understand how truly honest he was being. Bryan had sacrificed so much, and he'd done it alone. Never again would Justice allow either of them to suffer in silence.

Justice replaced his fingers with a soft kiss, worshiping the visible sign of his husband's mortality. He let his tongue taste the scar, reveling in the heat and flavor of fresh skin. He smoothed his hands against Bryan's shoulders and pushed him back toward the bed, never breaking their contact, falling on top of him, keeping their bodies touching at multiple points.

He trailed hot kisses down the ridges of Bryan's solid chest and abs. He might not have liked Herrera working with his husband, but he had to give the man credit where due. Bryan looked and felt just like Justice liked him, solid and hot as fuck.

He slid his hand down Bryan's torso taking a direct path to Bryan's straining cock. As his fingers slid beneath the elastic waistband of his underwear, Justice laughed. Within a few moments of Bryan putting them on they were already spotted with precum and on their way off of his body and on to the floor.

Justice kept his mouth locked on Bryan's, tasting him, sipping from him. It had been too long since he felt this connected to his man; he didn't want to let that go, not even for the temptation of tasting the heavy cock filling his palm.

This was about more than sex. All throughout their separation, Justice and Bryan never lost their physical love for one another. Thinking back on it, they'd spent just as much time sexing throughout the five years they'd been separated as they had their first sixteen years together. Granted, Justice was away for months at a time in the Marine Corps, but whenever they met, no matter how hurt or angry they were, no matter how insistent Bryan was that there would be no reconciliation, they'd never lost their desire for one another.

Sex was the easy part, after all their years together, they knew what the other wanted. Their bodies pretty much ran on autopilot. But in all that time they hadn't been able to reach each other's hearts.

Tonight, Justice felt Bryan deep down in his heart, through every tiny vessel of his being. Bryan was there, in his blood, spreading through his system like a warm elixir, rejuvenating his spirit, chasing the echoes away from his soul.

Bryan broke away from the desperate kiss, concern shadowing the love in his eyes.

"Are you all right? We don't have to do this."

Justice tightened his hand around Bryan's cock and savored the slow mewl that escaped his lips.

"I think we do," Justice countered.

Bryan closed his eyes. Justice could see the effect of his ministrations etched into the tight lines of Bryan's taut and trembling body.

"I think you know what I mean, Jussy."

He did. They'd said so much, revealed more in the last fifteen minutes than they had in the last five years. The rational thing to do would have been to keep the dialogue going, or at least allow some time to pass while everything settled in.

To hell with rational.

They'd spent too much time lost in a haze of misunderstanding. Now that they'd found this moment where they'd rediscovered their foundation, the thing that brought them together in the first place, their love for one another was the only thing Justice would allow either of them to focus on right now.

"Everything I need is right here." Justice flattened his lips to Bryan's. "You good with that?"

A wide grin pulled at the edges of Bryan's mouth. It was full and bright and it matched the sparkle growing in Bryan's eyes. This was how his man should always look. Loved…hopeful.

"Let me get what we need," Justice winked before quickly stepping away and praying they had enough supplies. A hurried pass of his hand at the bottom of the nightstand drawer yielded Justice exactly what they needed. Lube in hand, he headed back to the treasure waiting for him, spread out for his delight.

A few rapid moves and he was just as naked as Bryan. Too eager to be inside Bryan's heat, he poured an ample amount of the cool gel on his fingers, immediately touching it to Bryan's puckered flesh.

Bryan's sharp intake of breath brought a familiar smile to Justice's face.

"Dude, we've been using this shit for how long? You still can't find the time to warm that shit up before you touch me?" Bryan's total body shiver made Justice laugh. This was a fall back to the normal, back when they weren't burdened with so much tension and conflict. Back to when they connected without thought.

"How many years have I not warmed the lube? Don't you think you should be used to it by now? Stop bitching and let me in."

Justice made quick work of stretching Bryan, preparing him for their lovemaking. If he weren't in such need to be inside of his husband, Justice would take the time to…he had to stop lying right there. Long torture was Bryan's strong point. He'd build the fire between them in slow, almost painful ways. Justice was all about fire, guns blazing and blasting. Twenty-one years later and that shit hadn't changed.

Why fuck with a good thing?

He pressed the tip of his cock inside Bryan's opening and waited for what seemed like an eternity for Bryan to adjust. Once he felt Bryan's hands on his ass pulling him toward his goal, Justice slid inside Bryan's slick hole until balls met ass and he felt Bryan squeeze the ever-loving-fuck out of his dick with a series of tight spasms.

Cock pulsing, he buried deep in an ass molded to the ridges of his dick. Justice pulled back slowly, breath hissing between clenched teeth as he marveled at how good it felt to be inside Bryan again.

He glanced down and watched Bryan wrap his fingers around his own weeping cock. That was it for his restraint. He leaned over, positioning himself over Bryan. Arms locked, hips canted, he snapped forward, loving the lost-in-ecstasy look Bryan was wallowing in right now.

Hooking one of Bryan's legs over his meaty arm, he went to work. The pull and slide of Bryan's ass down his cock had his blood on fire. The love Bryan wove around his heart kept him tied to this man in ways he'd never be able to explain.

He'd hurt for and because of Bryan, and still, there was no one on the planet he'd rather give his heart to than the man moaning beneath him. Bryan had owned him from the first moment he smiled. He lived for that smile, ached to see it in its full splendor through the worst of their trying times.

"I'm close, Jussy. I just need…please," Bryan's moaning sending shocks of pleasure through Justice's system.

God that sound. It sparked fire in Justice's balls, tightening them, drawing them up. The electric zing of his climax was crashing down on him, he had to give them both what they needed. He slapped Bryan's hand out of the way and matched the long pulls on Bryan's dick with a piston like stroke of his hips.

The deep howl that poured out of Bryan let Justice know he was hitting his lover's prostate at just the right angle. A handful of strokes later and wet heat erupted from Bryan, hitting his chin and chest.

The sight of Bryan's spunk was the last of Justice's resolve. He planted both hands on Bryan's shoulders and pounded until liquid heat exploded from his balls, through his cock, and emptied into the latex covering his sputtering dick.

He fell directly on Bryan. Partly because that nut had robbed him of his control over his motor skills at that point, partly because he wanted nothing between them, not even air.

They rested there quietly, their breathing in perfect rhythm, their hearts in perfect synchronization. Justice was nearly lulled into rejuvenating sleep when he heard Bryan call his name.

"You know this isn't going to fix things?" Bryan's soft words were bathed in concern, not rejection, a fact Justice was more than grateful for.

Justice nodded. It wouldn't, no matter how much he wished it could, sex would never sustain them. But if this crazy connection between them couldn't keep them eternally linked Justice was afraid to ask the question lingering in his mind.

What would?

Chapter 13

He pulled Bryan into the enclosure of his arms. After going so long without Bryan, Justice needed to feel him, have him as near as possible.

"No, the sex won't fix anything; it's just a reminder of what we stand to lose if we don't work on this. I'm willing to put in the work if you are," Justice offered. "Don't know about you, but I need what we have in my life. I need to come home to this, to you. Not just for the sex, but all of it."

"Two conditions," Bryan's ultimatum briefly knocking Justice out of the comfort their embrace had gifted him. "The department assigned me a shrink when I was shot on the job. I want us to start going to couples therapy while you're home. If we have a chance at making us work, that's our best weapon."

Soothing relief poured over Justice, making him reach for Bryan again, pulling him closer into his chest. Justice wasn't opposed to therapy. He didn't exactly relish the idea of spilling his secrets to a complete stranger either, but he definitely saw the value in seeking help.

He'd been in the military long enough to witness firsthand what happened when service men and women didn't have a healthy outlet for all of the pain, torment, and ugliness they witnessed during their service. He wasn't about to let that kind of darkness consume either Bryan or himself.

"Fine, let me know when and where and I'll be there. What's your next condition?" Justice relaxed a little. The first stipulation hadn't been so bad. The second would probably be more of the same.

"You apologize to your sister and to Martin," Bryan's straight face and squinting eyes told Justice his husband wasn't joking.

Justice rolled his eyes. "Come on, man. Anything but that. You know if I apologize to True I will never live that shit down. And that fucking Herrera had anything I gave him coming. He had his fucking hands on my man. He was trying to kick it to my man in my face, in front of my damn family. He's lucky I didn't slit his fucking throat for his trouble."

Bryan pinched the bridge of his nose, a clear sign his patience was slipping away from him.

"That man was not trying to get at me, Justice. He's straight. The only thing he was doing was helping me get through the last leg of my rehab to get back to my job. He was being a friend while my husband was being an asshole."

"Fine," Justice felt his lips sink into a full pout. Yes he was a grown man, a Marine even, lying in his bed pouting over his husband's recriminations. His sister was always right. Telling her so wasn't going to do much for sucking the air out of her already over-inflated ego. "I'll apologize to him, but not True. She goaded me into this bullshit."

Bryan's body shook next to him in laughter. "She really did. I was convinced you'd see right through her plan, but you walked right into it full steam ahead."

"Trust me," Justice lifted a brow. "I knew she was baiting me. But once I saw that fucker with his hands all over you, I couldn't focus on True's bullshit. I just knew I had to get to my man before anyone else did."

"And you got him back," Bryan countered. "Which is why you should apologize to your sister. She was trying to help your marriage and you acted the ass. Make it right with her."

Justice turned to his side to face Bryan. He leaned in and Bryan met him halfway for a sweet kiss laced with just enough spice to make Justice's spent dick twitch with an attempt at excitement.

"Fine, I'll make it right with my sister."

Bryan rewarded his capitulation with a rough slide of his tongue on top of Justice's and a firm squeeze of his growing cock. Justice moaned into the kiss, his hips moving of their own accord to the rhythm Bryan's fist was creating.

"Don't let me go again, Bryan," Justice sighed his pleasure into their kiss, relishing the feel of his husband's taste, and the feel of Bryan's skin pressed against his own.

"We've taken each other through so many changes over the last five years. Just don't let any of them cause you to let me go again, I couldn't bear it."

"Love's changes will happen whether we want them too or not." Bryan's resigned tone stirred uncertainty in Justice's belly. "But that's what love is; change, evolution, growth. If we don't change, don't adapt, we die, it dies. No matter what change our love brings our way, I can promise you, I will never allow it to separate us again."

Bryan kissed Justice again and tightened his grip on Justice's cock, sending thrills of anticipation to his aching balls.

"Oh, baby," the sinister curve of Bryan's lips giving away the devilish nature of his unspoken thoughts. "With a cock this pretty, you never have to worry about me letting you go again.

"God I love you," Justice pumped his hips trying his best to get Bryan to do more than just admire his cock.

"I know, now shut up and show me."

Justice looked up at the brightness of Bryan's smile and realized why he'd always loved it. That smile tethered him, gave Justice an anchor in a world that was filled with too many uncertainties. Bryan's smile was security.

They'd almost allowed death and pride to destroy that smile.

Thank God for a meddling sister.

A fact he would never utter in the presence of another person, especially said meddling sister.

The shrill ring of a specific ringtone pulled him out of Bryan's warmth, his mind instantly fastening onto the unique sound.

Speak of the devil.

He knew who was calling, and if his sister was calling him on this phone from that ringtone, he knew why.

Justice sat up and reached for the offending device.

"Amare," his succinct tone informing his caller he was ready and able to accept whatever information she had to give.

"Our friends in Azuria need our help," True's calm voice slid over the line revealing no indication of just how severe this new development was. Justice didn't need her to. Whenever their team was called on a mission, it was only the worst of the worst situations waiting for them. "Report to JFK, I'll text the terminal and gate info. Wheels up in sixty."

"Hard copy," Justice's voice was equally calm and detached. He clicked the call to a silent end and turned his attention to Bryan, preparing to placate him.

"Duty calls?" Bryan sat up straight against the headboard.

"Yeah, at the most inopportune time too. We're just beginning to sort things out."

"Well, that's what happens when our jobs call, we have to answer. Fortunately your husband isn't only a police lieutenant, but a former Marine as well. I get it. I'm not thrilled about it, but I get it."

Bryan kissed him, marking Justice, imprinting himself onto Justice's senses. "Now go on to wherever it is you need to go, kick ass when you get there, and bring yourself back to me, Marine. You got that?"

"Oorah, Lieutenant Amare," Justice gave Bryan a quick kiss and a smile. "Oorah!"

The End

Author Bio

LaQuette is an erotic, multicultural romance author of M/F and M/M love stories. Her writing style brings intellect to the drama. She often crafts emotionally epic, fantastical tales that are deeply pigmented by reality's paintbrush. Her novels are filled with a unique mixture of savvy, sarcastic, brazen, and unapologetically sexy characters who are confident in their right to appear on the page.

This bestselling Erotic Romance Author is the 2016 Author of the Year Golden Apple Award Winner, 2016 Write Touch Award Winner for Best Contemporary Mid-length Novel, 2016 Swirl Awards 1st Place Winner in Romantic Suspense, and 2016

Aspen Gold Award Finalist in Erotic Romance. LaQuette—a native of Brooklyn, New York—spends her time catering to her three distinct personalities: Wife, Mother, and Educator.

Writing—her escape from everyday madness—has always been a friend and source of comfort. At the age of sixteen she read her first romance novel and realized the genre was missing something: people that looked and lived like her. As a result, her characters and settings are always designed to provide positive representations of people of color and various marginalized communities.

She loves hearing from readers and discussing the crazy characters that are running around in her head causing so much trouble. Contact her on Facebook, Twitter, @LaQuetteLikes, her website, www.NovelsbyLaQuette.com, Amazon, her Facebook group, LaQuette's Lounge, Instagram, @la_quette, and via email at LaQuette@NovelsbyLaQuette.com.

.

Newsletter Signup

Hello,

If you're interested in staying current with all of the happenings with my writing, previews, and giveaways, sign up for my monthly newsletter by visiting http://bit.ly/2o0XZ7n

Love's Dangers

A Losing My Way Novella

by

LaQuette

Coming This Fall...

Martin Herrera has spent twenty years in the Marine Corps doing what Uncle Sam ordered him to and loving every minute of it. Well...almost every minute of it. There were definitely things he wouldn't have chosen to do, things he wished so badly he could take back, or at the very least, forget.

Apocalyptic memories from a desert hell chased him off of the battlefield and into physiotherapy first as a patient, and then as a provider. Since then, his work life has been all about helping his fellow Marines get their bodies and minds right to walk back on the field.

He's content. Considering all he's done and seen, that's more than he can ask for. His marriage ripped apart by deployment and ignorance, Martin has decided the only commitment he can handle is to his patients and his work. Frequent trips to whatever local pickup places he finds himself near are all he needs to find companionship. Anything else and he doesn't have time for it. At least that's his resolution until a sexy, Marine walks into his world needing his help.

Julien Hargrove is a Marine temporarily stationed at 6th Comm in Brooklyn, NY, as he heals from an injury. When his commanding officer sends him to a recently retired Marine who now practices rehab therapy in the civilian world, Julien is both grateful and scared out of his mind.

Martin is knowledgeable, and confident, and his commanding bedside manner makes Julien want to do just about anything the older Marine demands. After fighting to break free of a power-hungry ex who mistook dominance for abuse, Julien quickly decides

Herrera is off limits. Too bad his body refuses to cooperate with that decree.

When Julien's ex resurfaces, will Martin look beyond his own pain and help his lover? Will Julien realize there's no weakness in needing help? Or will they both accept the dangers of love as a reason or a barrier to being together?

Other Titles by LaQuette

Queens of Kings: Books 1-4 on Amazon